Appointment with Death

The arrow flashed across the clearing and hit the grinning assassin in the back between the shoulder blades. It punched its way through him, thrusting its wickedly barbed head out of his chest in a shower of blood.

He fell, flopping facedown. His groan became a death rattle . . .

Behind the body, some bushes parted and a man carrying a crossbow stepped into view. A big American, tall, dark, and lethal.

He was Nick Carter.

The Killmaster had kept his rendezvous.

NICK CARTER IS IT!

FROM THE NICK CARTER
KILLMASTER SERIES

NICK CARTER

KILLMASTER

Holy War

C

CHARTER BOOKS, NEW YORK

HOLY WAR

A Charter Book / published by arrangement with
The Condé Nast Publications, Inc.

PRINTING HISTORY
Charter edition / May 1987

ISBN: 0-441-57294-4

Charter Books are published by The Berkley Publishing Group,
200 Madison Avenue, New York, New York 10016.

PRINTED IN THE UNITED STATES OF AMERICA

*Dedicated to the men of the
Secret Services of the
United States of America*

ONE

The Golden Temple Massacre occurred in Punjab state in June 1984, when Prime Minister Indira Gandhi ordered the Indian army to oust well-armed militants from the Sikhs' holiest shrine. Over two thousand Sikhs were killed in that action. Soon after, Mrs. Gandhi was assassinated by Sikhs in her personal bodyguard. Vengeful Hindu mobs joined with criminal gangs to torture, plunder, and murder hundreds of Sikh men, women, and children.

Somehow the unrest was quelled, order was restored, and the citizens of the world's biggest democracy settled into a sullen, uneasy peace. India had survived its latest crisis.

The next time, it might not be so lucky.

The struggle to stop a second Golden Temple bloodbath began on a suffocatingly hot Benares midnight in

June. Guptil Gucharvi kept a lonely vigil on the right bank and the wrong side of the river Ganges.

Guptil was short, stocky, owlish. The hair at his temples was prematurely gray. More than a few of those gray hairs were souvenirs of past adventures with the man he was scheduled to meet very soon.

He wore a loose-fitting white cotton short-sleeved shirt, dark baggy trousers, and sandals. Stuffed in his pants pocket was a small-caliber pistol. From time to time he patted it, reassuring himself that it was still there.

The Ganges is sacred, and holiest of all its precincts are those waters that lap the shores of the world's oldest continually occupied city, Varanasi, known to Westerners as Benares. Hindus hold that to die in Benares is truly heaven. Those fortunate enough to expire in the holy city will instantly transcend to an eternity of pure bliss. Every day, from all corners of the subcontinent, thousands of aged pilgrims come to the city to die.

Benares is situated on the river's left bank. The Hindus also believe that he who dies on the river's right bank will be reborn as a jackass.

Guptil Gucharvi maintained his watch on the right bank. Long-abandoned crumbling terraces tumbled in stepped layers down to the oily, sluggish river. Lush masses of tropical foliage smothered the slope. The green labyrinth was honeycombed by a network of paths, walks, game trails, and rat runs.

The mini-jungle had all but reclaimed the terrace where Guptil stood. The overgrown granite oblong lay two thirds of the way down from the riverbank's flat summit, where his car was hidden. Gaps in the brush gave him a panoramic vista of the river and the city, a splended view that nonetheless failed to enchant him. The boat for which he was keenly watching had still not appeared.

Guptil consulted his wristwatch. It was now a quarter

past twelve and his contact was late.

Something rustled in the brush behind him.

Guptil, startled, slapped his hand on his pistol. He was no gunman. He was an expediter, a fixer, a cutter of red tape, a man who made things happen. Still, he was glad he had the gun. All day and night, he'd had the feeling that he was being followed.

After a pause, the rustling noises resumed. They sounded near, no more than a stone's throw away. The movements were too loud to have been made by river rats, even the huge local variety.

A wild dog, perhaps?

Somewhere in the bushes a twig snapped.

Guptil hauled his pistol from his pocket, dropped into a crouch, and froze.

The foliage was too thick to see through. For all he knew, a small army could be lurking behind that impenetrable wall of vegetation.

Guptil listened hard. His quick breaths rasped like two rough boards rubbed together. A fat drop of sweat rolled down his nose, splattering on the stones.

A small swift creature burst out of the underbrush—long, low, and agile to the point of fluidity.

A mongoose!

Startled, Guptil jerked the trigger of his pistol, but nothing happened.

The mongoose scuttled over Guptil's feet, across the terrace, and out of sight.

Laughing nervously, Guptil checked his pistol. It had not fired because he had neglected to throw off the safety catch.

Well, he'd be the first to admit he was no expert with firearms. And to think that a little mongoose had nearly panicked him into a shooting spree. Guptil shook his head and looked again toward the sacred Ganges. He never thought to wonder what might have spooked the animal into breaking its cover.

A few minutes later, the sounds he'd been longing to hear came from the river: the muffled splashing of oars, and the creak of oarlocks. A narrow skiff was being rowed to shore. Guptil's contact had arrived.

Guptil stuffed the pistol back into his pocket and went to meet the man. A stepped path, weed-choked and vine-strewn, slanted down to the water's edge. Guptil walked with care, fearful of poisonous snakes. The steep path was hemmed by trees, bushes, and lianas. The foliage walled him in, blocking his view of the shore.

When he finally completed his descent, he saw the shallow-draft skiff beached on the muddy bank. But his contact was nowhere to be seen.

Guptil's ready greeting died unspoken. He prowled up and down the shore but saw no sign of the man. His low-voiced, urgent calls received an equal lack of response.

Guptil scratched his head. The boat hadn't rowed itself across the water. Yet its occupant had utterly vanished, as if swallowed up by the night and the river.

A solution of sorts came to Guptil. Many paths and trails rose from the river to the terrace. Perhaps his contact had climbed one of them while Guptil made his descent, and they had unknowingly passed one another. Sighing, Guptil turned and went back up the path.

Going up was far more difficult than walking down because of the extreme angle of the slope. Grabbing onto creepers and branches, Guptil hauled himself up.

Thrashing and grunting like a water buffalo in a cane brake, Guptil clambered to the terrace. When he reached it, he was a wreck. His clothes were sweat-soaked. His left sandal clung to his foot by a single thong. Unused to such exertion, he clung panting to a tree, unsure whether he would throw up, pass out, or suffer a heart attack.

His agonies were forgotten when somebody grabbed his arm.

"Carter!" Guptil gasped. "Am I glad to see you!"

That same somebody shoved a gun muzzle against Guptil's skull. "Don't move."

"Who are you?" Guptil asked. This was not the man he had come to meet.

The unknown assailant rapped Guptil's head with the pistol barrel. "Keep still."

Stunned, Guptil clutched the tree to keep from falling. For a moment he saw double, then his vision came back into focus.

The man frisked him quickly. Guptil recoiled from his touch. The gunman pressed his weapon's muzzle against the underside of Guptil's chin, forcing his head back. "I said, keep still!"

Guptil froze. The man fished out Guptil's pistol and pocketed it. More confident now that Guptil was disarmed, he took a few steps back, and Guptil finally had a chance to take a look.

His wiry opponent couldn't have weighed more than 125 pounds soaking wet. His bony face was all angles and wedges, with brilliantined black hair swept back into a rooster's crest. He wore cheap, flashy clothes, and twitched and fidgeted like a dope addict.

Guptil didn't know him, but he knew the type. The fellow was a *goondah*, a vicious petty criminal, a hoodlum. A small-time punk, yes, but his long-barreled gun was larger than life.

The gunman grinned, his face lighting up with a crocodilelike smile. His wiry form squirmed with restless energy. Even standing still, he seemed to swagger.

"You gave me a bad time for a while. I thought we'd lost you," he said.

"Who are you?" Guptil asked again. "What do you want?"

"I want to take your life."

"You—you're crazy!"

His opponent was enjoying himself. "I'm Shaheed. I tell you that because it's only fair that you know the name of the man who's going to kill you."

"Kill me? Why?"

"You shouldn't have meddled in things that don't concern you," Shaheed said.

Guptil keyed up his nerve for a mad plunge into the brush. Even if he caught a slug or two, he still might make his getaway.

"Don't give me any trouble, unless you want to die hard," Shaheed said.

At this close range Shaheed could hardly miss. Guptil sagged into quivering uncertainty.

Somebody was stumbling around on the slope above the terrace. Guptil tried to pretend he hadn't heard anything, but he needn't have bothered. Shaheed heard it, too, but it didn't alarm him.

"That's my partner," he told Guptil. "We'll wait for him. He'd be so very angry if he wasn't in on the kill."

Shaheed called his partner's name: "Eckar!"

"Shaheed!" a hoarse voice replied. "Where are you?"

"Down here!"

"Where? I can't see you!"

"Take the path and come down here," Shaheed said. "I have our man!"

"Good work! Is he alive?"

"Yes," Shaheed said and chuckled, "but not for long, so hurry up!"

"I'll be right there! Don't start without me!"

"I won't, but hurry!"

Eckar's movement toward them could easily be tracked by the noise he made. Then, suddenly, he cried out in pain.

"Curse these thorn bushes! They're tearing me to shreds!"

"Stop being such a woman and get down here!" Shaheed snapped.

"I can't find the path!"

"Just keep going the way you're going."

"Right! I see it now," Eckar said.

Shaheed and Guptil still couldn't see Eckar. There was more crashing and thrashing in the bush.

Suddenly a sound rang out, a twanging not unlike that of the bass string of an electric guitar being plucked, but deeper and more resonant.

"What was that?" Now it was Shaheed's turn to be startled. "Eckar?" They could no longer hear Eckar making his way through the undergrowth.

Keeping his gun trained on Guptil, Shaheed prowled the border of tangled vegetation, calling his partner's name with increasing vexation. "Eckar, where are you? Why don't you speak? Eckar! *Eckar!*"

No reply.

Shaheed wasn't smiling his reptilian grin anymore.

"Maybe he fell in a hole and broke his neck," Guptil suggested.

"If he did, it won't save yours," Shaheed snapped. His gun maintained its steady bead on Guptil, offering him no chance to make a break.

Guptil had the feeling that Shaheed had just reached a decision, and the outcome, for himself, would be most unpleasant.

"Can we—can we make a deal?" Guptil asked.

"No." The thrill of imminent murder restored Shaheed's hideous grin. He loved to pull the trigger. "Prepare to die!"

Suddenly something flashed across the clearing and hit Shaheed in the back between the shoulder blades. A narrow shaft punched its way through him, thrusting its wickedly barbed head out of his chest in a shower of blood.

Shaheed screamed and dropped his gun. His hands moved jerkily around the dripping arrowhead protruding from his shattered breastbone.

He fell, flopping facedown. The arrow was jammed back into his chest and protruded further from his back. Shaheed's groan became a death rattle. A few kicks, a convulsion, and he was dead.

Behind the body, some bushes parted and a man carrying a crossbow stepped into view. A big American, tall, dark, and lethal.

He was Nick Carter.

The Killmaster had kept his rendezvous.

Thirty-six hours earlier, Carter had been dangling on a rope over a 1,500-foot-deep chasm in Iceland, playing cat-and-mouse games with a KGB agent. He'd barely had time to shake off the chill before he was en route to India. He made the last leg of the journey by a commercial flight, and his plane had been delayed for five hours because of a bomb threat. Two weeks earlier, an Air India jet blew up in midair, killing 332 passengers and crew members. The Khalistan Commando Force, a radical Sikh terror group, claimed credit for the blast.

The delay was hardly an auspicious start for his trip, but he had made it to India all in one piece. Of course, leaving that way was the challenge.

Benares was almost unbearably hot and humid. Carter felt as if he were taking a steambath while wearing his Icelandic sweaters. Still, it was nothing compared to the heat that Hawk was putting on him for some fast results.

David Hawk was the white-haired, cigar-chomping boss of AXE, the supersecret U.S. government agency that handled—as quietly as possible—covert actions deemed critically important to the national security.

Hawk answered to a very few people, one of them the President. He wouldn't hesitate to tell any or all of them where to get off if he thought they were wrong. That was why Hawk stayed in power, though administrations came and went. He told them what they had to hear, not what they wanted to hear.

Hawk was also a master strategist who shuttled his agents around the world as if they were human pieces on a global chessboard. And Nick Carter, designated Agent N3, was his premier Killmaster, which made Carter the logical candidate to avenge the Delhi strike.

The U.S. maintains an embassy in Delhi. Salted among the State Department types are a number of CIA operatives working the local beat. A few days earlier, five such agents failed to report for work.

They all worked in the same unit and the group leader was among the missing. The outfit was strictly CIA, posing as a bureaucratic fiefdom among the diplomats. Overnight, the staffers vanished into thin air.

But AXE had learned that there had been a witness to the mysterious disappearance, and that's how Carter found himself sweltering in Benares.

Carter had worked in India before, but he didn't consider himself an old India hand. But Guptil Gucharvi was. This was his turf. Carter put Guptil on the case.

With his insider's connections, it didn't take Guptil very long to locate the witness. Carter arranged to meet Guptil on the right bank of the Ganges at a secluded spot he'd used before.

Carter never walked blindly into anything; he always checked out the lay of the land first. When his skiff grounded, Carter leaped ashore and melted into the shadows. He wanted to have a look around.

His moves were good; no one heard him prowl. But he heard and saw Shaheed and Eckar. One glance was enough to make him suspicious.

When Shaheed found Guptil, Carter had a problem.

He had to take out Eckar without goading Shaheed into blasting Guptil. He had no silencer for his gun, so shooting Eckar was out. The undergrowth was too tangled for him to rush Eckar and neutralize him with a karate chop or some adroit knifework.

Carter's newest toy supplied an elegant solution. It was a Power-Slam crossbow pistol, complete with a steel-spring bow and a cable bowstring. Even with the hand-held "goat's-foot" cocking device, it took plenty of muscle to draw the bowstring. Fired at a fifty-foot distance from the target, the weapon could propel a six-inch steel-headed bolt through a one-inch-thick pine board.

The noise that had so mystified Shaheed and Guptil was the sound of the crossbow vibrating after a bolt was discharged.

Eckar was made of stuff considerably less dense than a pine board. The razor-barbed bolt drilled him clear through and kept on going. One down, one to go.

Carter fitted a new bolt to his crossbow, sneaked behind Shaheed, and waited for his shot. And that had been that.

Nick Carter stuck his foot under Shaheed and flipped him over. The face meant nothing to him. "Who is he?"

"I don't know," Guptil said. "Shaheed, he said his name was. A cheap *goondah*, a hired hand."

"Hired by whom?"

"By somebody who doesn't want you to meet your precious witness," Guptil said. "The game is getting rough."

He went down on one knee beside the body. His gun jutted out of the top of Shaheed's trousers, and Guptil reclaimed it. "I'll need this."

He eyed Shaheed's pistol, a large-caliber, big-bore automatic. It packed a lot more punch than his own gun. He pocketed his gun and held on to Shaheed's. "This may come in handy. After all, a man can't have too many guns."

"My sentiments exactly," Carter said as he turned out Shaheed's pockets and inspected their contents, discovering a fat wad of bank notes. "Nice piece of change, especially for a two-bit punk. He must have been paid in advance for killing you." He tossed Guptil the billfold of rupees. "Combat pay."

"All gratuities cheerfully accepted, sahib," Guptil joked, pocketing the money. AXE paid very well, but any extra was appreciated.

Apart from the money, Carter's search uncovered nothing of interest. He stood up and turned to Guptil. "Where's your car?"

"Not far from here. I hope those *goondahs* didn't sabotage it."

"If they did, we'll steal theirs," Carter said. "Come on, let's move. And stop waving that gun around, for crissakes! You're making me nervous."

Guptil scoffed. "You haven't got a nervous bone in your body."

TWO

Guptil's car was a battered but serviceable white sedan. Before starting it up, Carter and Guptil gave it a thorough going-over to make sure that nobody had rigged a bomb to it.

"Where to?" Carter asked.

"Mulag Gaol."

"The witness is in jail? He's in some sort of protective custody?"

"Not exactly." Guptil chuckled. "She's under arrest for theft, resisting an officer, and provoking a riot."

"She?"

"Didn't you know the witness is a woman?"

"I didn't have much time for background," Carter admitted.

"In that case, let me be the first to tell you that you're buying a real prize package. I did some checking on our star performer, Miss Vashti Takore. The Takore clan is not unknown in Delhi and neither is Miss Vashti. Like the rest of her family, Miss Vashti is a *malka-sansi*." He glanced at Carter. "You know what that is, Nick? A *malka-sansi*?"

"I think so. Some kind of a thief, right?"

"That's putting it mildly. It's a hereditary caste of thieves whose members are born and bred to the robber's trade. They consort with thieves, marry thieves, and raise their children to be thieves. My contacts in the Delhi police tell me that the Takores are skilled practitioners of their profession. Or at least they were."

"Why the past tense?" Carter asked.

"Because the Takores were netted in a police raid two nights ago and are all under arrest in Delhi. Quite a coincidence, don't you think?"

"I don't believe in coincidences," Carter said.

"In this case I agree with you, Nick. But it's a stroke of luck for us. If the Takores were at large, their sister wouldn't be in Mulag Gaol, waiting for a white knight to come to her rescue."

"How soon will we get there?"

"Soon," Guptil said, driving through the dark city, "soon."

Carter flipped open the lid of his cigarette case. "Smoke?"

"Thank you, yes."

They lit up, both enjoying the custom-blended tobacco, one of Carter's personal indulgences.

Carter was well aware of the Surgeon General's proclamation that smoking was hazardous to one's health. But the Surgeon General didn't have to go dodging down dark alleys playing life-and-death games with foreign agents, hired thugs, Middle Eastern terrorists, and a host of other equally deadly opponents.

Carter figured that when he reached the age of fifty

he'd think about quitting smoking. If he reached age fifty. No Killmaster had yet.

Guptil's car wasn't followed. Shaheed and Eckar must have been working without backup, a pair of *goondah* triggermen looking to make a quick kill.

It was a rugged ride. The old car and bad roads combined to give Carter a hell of a shaking. The car's springs and shocks might have been made out of rubber bands for all the good they did.

Presently they entered a sprawling district south of the city proper, a marshy flatland crisscrossed with abandoned railroad tracks. Long, low, barrackslike buildings housed weaving mills, dyers' plants, and other aspects of the textile trade. Judging from the shabby, run-down condition of the neighborhood, business was not exactly booming.

Ahead rose the gray walls of Mulag Gaol. The grim, castlelike prison had its origin as a fort built by a Mogul lord in 1689. Since then, renovations and repairs to the stone structure had been minimal. Apart from such modern necessities as searchlights, barbed wire, and machine guns, the fortress remained virtually unchanged since it was first built.

Mulag Gaol housed both male and female prisoners, and Guptil halted the car in front of the gate to the women's section.

"Everything is taken care of," Guptil assured Carter. "I'll go tell the guard we're here, and then we'll drive right in."

Guptil got out of the car and walked up to the massive gate of iron grillwork. A uniformed guard came out of the gatehouse to meet him.

Carter could see Guptil clearly in the car's headlights. The Indian began waving his arms angrily and shouting through the bars at the guard. The guard shouted back. Carter's Hindustani was rudimentary but he didn't need an interpreter to know that the two Indians were having more than a slight disagreement.

Abruptly, Guptil threw up his hands and stalked back to the car. He stuck his head through the driver's side window and said breathlessly, "This is intolerable! It's an outrage! The guard I bribed to let us in tonight didn't show up for duty, and his idiotic replacement claims he knows nothing about the arrangement!"

"Don't you have a higher-up on the payroll?"

"Indeed, yes! The deputy warden himself. He'd let us in in a minute, but I can't reach him without going through this idiot first."

"I guess he'll have to be greased too," Carter sighed. It was too hot to get angry. "How much is this going to cost?"

Guptil shook his head. "The reputation of Guptil Gucharvi is on the line. I told you we'd get in, and we will. I'll pay him myself."

"Well, thanks."

"Quite all right. You can reimburse me later."

Guptil returned to the gate, reached into his pocket, pulled out the billfold of rupees lifted from Shaheed, and passed half the cash through the grillwork to the guard.

"You'll get the rest when we're inside," Guptil said.

"As you will, sahib. It shall be done at once," the guard said.

Guptil was soon back in the driver's seat. The ponderous gate was unlocked and opened. Guptil drove under the archway and into a square, dimly lit courtyard. The gate clanged shut.

An ambulance was parked at the side, its motor idling. Two white-uniformed attendants sat in its cab, smoking and talking.

Even before Guptil's car rolled to a halt, the guard from the gate showed up with his hand out. Guptil slapped the rest of the rupees into his palm.

"Thank you, sahib," the guard said and grinned broadly.

"Bah!"

Carter and Guptil got out of the car. While seeming to look in another direction, Carter eyed the ambulance. Appearances could be deceiving, he knew, but the vehicle's occupants struck him as a pair of tough cookies— glowering, beetle-browed *goondahs*.

"Ask the guard what that ambulance is doing here," he said to Guptil.

Guptil quizzed the guard in Hindustani. "A doctor and nurse are examining an inmate who might have cholera," he explained to Carter. "If she does, she'll have to be removed immediately." Guptil shuddered. "You can imagine how fast that would spread in this prison. Like wildfire!"

"Do public health officials usually make their visits this late at night?"

Guptil shrugged. "I suppose they do if it's something this serious. A cholera epidemic would be terrible!"

Before Carter could press the matter, a second guard stepped out of the gatehouse. Guptil glanced at the newcomer, then did a double take when he recognized him.

"That's the guard I made the arrangement with!" Guptil confronted the first guard. "You told me that he was off duty tonight!"

Straight-faced, the guard replied, "I was mistaken."

"Mistaken? Hah! You lied! You planned this so you could squeeze more money out of me!"

The guard shrugged. "You paid him, but you didn't pay me. So I evened things up. What could be more fair?"

"If you think you can get away with this, you are very much mistaken indeed! Give me—"

Carter grabbed Guptil's arm and steered him away. "You won't get anywhere with these shakedown artists, so save your breath."

Blandly smiling, the guard motioned toward a door. "Please go right in. Deputy Warden Dutta is expecting you."

Carter hustled the furious Guptil inside, his own mind racing and his sixth sense on full alert.

A public health inspection at Mulag Gaol at 1:30 A.M.?

Carter didn't buy it.

THREE

Vashti Takore could not sleep, but insomnia was a blessing for which she was profoundly grateful. The last seventy-two hours had been a waking nightmare that showed no signs of ending, but far worse were the visions haunting her when she slept. For when she slept, she dreamed.

She dreamed of Narayan, her brother, and the way he looked when last she saw him, in a back booth at the Club Blib in Delhi.

Three days earlier, Vashti had prowled the dens and dives and fleshpots of Delhi's Connaught Circle vice district, searching for Narayan. Had it been only three days? she wondered. It was hard to keep track of time from a windowless cell in Mulag Gaol.

Narayan was a fool, and when he was drunk, he was a bigger fool. He had been rip-roaring drunk that night in

19

Delhi, according to acquaintances who had seen him making his unsteady rounds of the bar circuit.

Narayan knew a secret. And when drunk, Narayan talked. He would talk himself into his grave if he wasn't careful, Vashti knew. As the night wore on, her search for him grew more and more frantic.

The sprawling vice district was rowdy, raucous, and dangerous. Even the whores generally worked in pairs for their own protection. Vashti searched alone. She had to. The rest of her family was hard at work; they'd been planning a job for months, and this was the night they were going to pull it off.

Vashti was a shapely beauty in her mid-twenties. A mane of glossy ebony hair, shimmering with midnight-blue highlights, trailed down to the small of her back. Her face was wide, heart-shaped, exquisitely molded, with dark brown eyes and succulent lips. Her stunning body, with its heavy bosom, narrow waist, and wide hips, could have served as a model for one of the Hindu goddesses whose voluptuous forms are carved in relief on many an ancient temple.

But Vashti was very much a modern woman. Her Western attire of a tight T-shirt and tighter jeans only accented her provocative form. And no less provocative to the legions of men swarming the district was her single, unescorted status. A lone female in the Circle district was surely a whore! Or else she was just looking for it. Either way, she was fair game, or so thought the young men who followed her.

But this stray cat had tiger claws—the local equivalent of brass knuckles, bristling with razor-sharp dagger points. The damage they could inflict with a single swipe was awesome. Brandishing them was usually enough to discourage all but the most insistent.

Vashti had already used them once that evening, when a foul-breathed drunk grabbed her and shoved her against a wall. One pass of the claws across a groping hand ribboned it with five deep slashes.

The drunk stared stupidly at his mutilated hand for a minute, watching it bleed. The pain finally percolated through to his pickled brain and he fled, howling, trailed by the derisive laughter of amused onlookers.

A sharp snap of her wrist flicked most of the blood from the claws. The rest she wiped clean with a handkerchief as she resumed her search. An hour passed, two, then three with no results.

"Pssst! Vashti!"

Vashti whirled around, unable to see who had called her name.

"Over here," the voice called.

A figure stood sheltered in a recessed doorway, out of the flow of pedestrian traffic. Shadow obscured him. Tightening her grip on the tiger claws, Vashti approached him.

"It's me, Jaswant!"

Jaswant was a petty crook who had eyes for her. Vashti relaxed—but just a little.

"Why are you hiding in the doorway?" she asked him.

"I don't want to be seen talking to you."

"Why not?"

"I just came from the Hamyun Café. Narayan's there."

"Thank God! I've been looking everywhere for him!"

"Well, he's there, all right. He's got a strange story to tell, and he's telling it to anybody who buys him a drink," Jaswant said. "The tale he's telling, Vashti, I didn't want to hear. Some things are too dangerous to know. You'd better find him before someone else does."

Vashti was off and running. When she reached the

Hamyun Café, her brother was gone. As she left the café, a rag-clad street urchin tugged at her arm.

"Miss Takore?" the emaciated child said slowly.

"Who are you? What do you want?" There was something unnerving about this hollow-eyed bundle of rags and bones saying her name.

"Narayan told me to watch for you," he said.

"Where is he?"

"He is waiting for you at the Club Blib."

"I never heard of the place," Vashti said.

Blank-eyed, the child just stared at her until she asked, "Well, where is it?"

"Aiyat Street."

"I know Aiyat Street. There's no club there."

"Follow me," the little boy said. "I will take you there."

The noisy crowds and bars and discos of Connaught Circle were soon left far behind. Aiyat Street was a dingy cul-de-sac, the last stop before the grave for the most used-up whores and burnt-out addicts. Its squalid brick buildings concealed untold human misery behind their crumbling façades.

The urchin shuffled into an alley. At its mouth, an ancient beggar squatted on his haunches. He stank so badly, Vashti gave him a wide berth. He ignored the intruders. He was so far gone, he was probably not even aware of them.

Vashti halted. "Are you sure this is the right place?"

The boy indicated an oblong hole fronting a blank brick wall in the middle of the alley. "Down there."

The hole was a stairwell leading down to a cellar door. Vashti circled it, peering down into the blackness. The door was outlined by yellow light leaking through the doorframe. Muffled music wafted up from below. When she looked up, her young guide was gone.

After some hesitation, she descended the narrow

flight of stone steps. The stairwell reeked of urine. Vashti gripped the tiger claws for reassurance.

Her free hand knocked on the door. She banged on the door until her small fist ached. She'd just turned around to go, when a small square hatch opened in the door at eye level. A pair of bloodshot, unfocused eyes looked out.

"Is this the Club Blib?" Vashti asked. "I'm supposed to meet my—"

The peephole hatch slid shut. Vexed, Vashti started up the stairs.

The door opened. The doorman said, "It's here." He was so decrepit he resembled a walking corpse. His withered brown hand beckoned Vashti within.

She took a deep breath, and entered. A tiny antechamber opened into a broad, low-ceilinged cellar. The air was stale and the walls dust-furred. A black puddle collected on the floor below a leaky overhead pipe.

Four tables with three chairs each occupied the center of the room. The chairs were unoccupied, except for one at a table to Vashti's left. A man sat slumped in it. His arms were folded on the tabletop and his head was pillowed on them. He snored steadily.

A filthy counter stood near the rear wall. Old, dark brown bottles were ranged along its top. An ancient Bakelite radio stood next to them, the source of the music Vashti had heard earlier.

To the left of the counter, a beaded curtain hung at the entrance to a narrow hallway lit by a red bulb. A row of wooden booths was ranged along the right wall. At first glance they seemed unoccupied.

Then she saw that the one farthest from her had someone in it. The booths were high-backed, so she could only see the top of a black-haired head.

She glanced over her shoulder. The old doorman sat perched on a wooden stool, reading a prayer book. A pair of wire-rimmed spectacles perched on the middle of his nose. He held the book in both hands, holding it close to his dim eyes. He seemed harmless enough. Vashti started forward.

Narayan sat in the last booth, out cold. Relief warred with rage in Vashti, relief at finding her brother and rage at his being in such a disgraceful condition.

He sat wedged in the corner, head turned away from her. He stank of booze, and worse. Vashti grabbed his shoulder to give him a good shaking.

"Narayan!"

She yanked him toward her. There was no resistance. He was limp as a rag doll. His curly head lolled over to one side, exposing his purple face.

His sightless eyes bulged, his mouth gaped, his blackened tongue protruded. Buried deep in his neck, almost hidden, was the instrument of execution, a golden cord. Narayan had been strangled to death.

Vashti's lips parted, but her throat seemed paralyzed.

A fat woman appeared from behind the counter where she'd been hiding and crept up behind Vashti. She moved with surprising stealth for one of her gross bulk. Vashti didn't know she was there until it was almost too late.

Sensing motion behind her, Vashti started to turn. She glimpsed an enormously fat woman bearing down on her. Brawny arms wrapped Vashti in a crushing bear hug.

The fat woman swung her around, overturning a chair. The man who'd been snoring at the table stood up. He was tall and thin, with sad, heavy-lidded eyes and an overgrown handlebar mustache. His shoulders shook and he wheezed with laughter. Then there was a golden cord in his hands and he laughed harder.

The monstrous arms held Vashti even more tightly, and the young woman couldn't get enough breath in her lungs to scream.

The doorman marked his place, closed his prayer book, and put it aside. He got off his stool and walked slowly toward them.

The sad-eyed thin man played with the golden cord, caressing it. "Careful, Primala. You'll break her." He didn't sound overly concerned.

"I won't break her. I'll just bend her a little," answered the fat woman.

"Bend her forward, so I can get my *ruhmal* around her pretty little neck."

The doorman kept on coming, but it was taking him a long time to get there.

The sad-eyed man held the cord between his fists. "Here's a necklace for you, my pet, a lovely golden necklace . . ."

Vashti lifted her right foot and brought the high heel down as hard as she could on Primala's foot, breaking the bones.

Primala screamed.

Vashti stomped again, grinding her heel until she heard more bones break. Primala screamed some more and broke her grip.

Vashti took a deep breath and burst free from Primala's arms. The sad-eyed man grabbed for her.

Vashti finally managed to put her tiger claws into play. She slashed out, ripping Sad-eyes across the throat. She must have cut a major artery, because suddenly blood was everywhere, a vivid burst of crimson in that old, dark brown cellar.

Sad-eyes clapped hands to what was left of his throat, but he couldn't hold back the blood. He folded at the knees and crouched on the floor.

Vashti ran for the door. The doorman tried to get out of her way. Her clawed hand lashed out, slapping his face, shredding the left side of it. Moaning, he slid down the wall and sat on the floor.

The door was barred and bolted. Vashti threw back

the bolts, but the bar was wedged tight.

Primala was coming toward her. Groaning, sobbing, cursing, the fat woman hobbled across the floor. She was moving pretty fast, too, despite her pain.

Vashti hammered the bar with the butt end of her tiger claw grip. She hit it a half-dozen times before it jarred loose.

Primala was a few paces away. Vashti threw the heavy bar at the angry woman's legs, knocking them out from under her. The fat woman fell, screaming her head off.

Vashti threw open the door and ran. She ran and ran and ran . . .

All the way to Benares and Mulag Gaol.

FOUR

Unlike the usual run of visitors to Mulag Gaol, Nick Carter was a paying customer. The guards didn't bother to search him or Guptil. Which was just as well, since the Killmaster was well armed.

Carter wore a tropical-weight beige sport coat, a pale blue cotton shirt, tan trousers, and a pair of brown loafers. The outfit had looked quite acceptable when he first stepped out of the air-conditioned jet that had brought him to India. Five minutes later, thanks to the tremendous heat and humidity of the pre-monsoon climate, Carter looked as if he'd taken a shower with his clothes on.

His jacket served more than the dictates of fashion, however. It concealed his 9mm Luger, holstered under his left armpit, and his stiletto, snug in its sheath on his right forearm. A few other surprises were planted on his person as well.

Deputy Warden Dutta received Carter and Guptil in the absent warden's office, which Dutta had commandeered during this night shift. Dutta was a square-faced, middle-aged man with a rather comical toothbrush mustache. There was something hauntingly familiar about him, although Carter had never met him before. Then, for a split second, Carter realized that Dutta bore an uncanny resemblance to Charlie Chaplin's portrayal of Hitler in his 1940 movie, *The Great Dictator*. He cast his eyes around the room to keep from smiling.

The administrative office was a scene of genial confusion. Relief of sorts from the oppressive heat was provided by the huge overhead fan. Every loose paper, file, and document in the room had to be weighted down to keep it from being blown away.

Guptil handled the introductions, describing Dutta as a "patriotic administrator who has been good enough to assist us in this delicate matter." Out of courtesy to Carter, and in acknowledgment that the bribes were AXE dollars, the conversation was conducted in English.

Vashti Takore's file was on the desk. Dutta consulted it.

He reviewed the charges. "The prisoner was apprehended in the act of picking the pocket of a Bombay pilgrim to our holy city. She put up quite a struggle, blackening the eye of one of the arresting officers. When finally under restraint, she then tried to incite a crowd of onlookers to prevent the officers from taking her away. Apparently, she was all too convincing. The crowd turned ugly and would not back down until the officers drew their guns."

Dutta shut the folder. "You realize that these are serious charges. We here in Varanasi do not look kindly on those who victimize pilgrims. Resisting arrest and inciting a riot are also most serious charges."

Deputy Warden Dutta grinned. "However, Mr. Gucharvi has convinced me that there are extenuating circumstances in this case."

It had taken no small amount of convincing. Buying the freedom of Vashti Takore had cost considerably more than a fistful of rupees. Guptil was happy that the reciprocal exchange of information between different police jurisdictions was in a primitive state. If Deputy Warden Dutta had known of Vashti's police record in Delhi, the price would really have soared.

Deputy Warden Dutta cleared his throat. "And now, I'm sure you gentlemen would like to take delivery of the prisoner and be on your way. So, if we could just finalize the arrangements . . ."

"Of course," Guptil said, and he passed Deputy Warden Dutta a bulging manila envelope.

"I beg you not to think I am casting any aspersions on your honest dealings, but I must count the money," Dutta said. "After all, if it should be short by some mistake, I could hardly apply to you for the outstanding sum later."

"No offense taken," Carter said. "But as you pointed out, we are in a hurry. We'd appreciate it if you could hasten our departure by having the prisoner brought here in the meantime."

"Certainly." Dutta activated the desk-top intercom and barked into it, but the machinery was on the blink and he couldn't communicate with his outer office. He bellowed at the top of his lungs for his subordinate.

His aide opened the door and stuck his head into the inner office. Dutta told him to have Vashti Takore brought to them.

"At once, sir."

Dutta resumed counting the cash. It was all there, of course; Guptil Gucharvi knew better than to give the deputy warden a short count within the walls of his prison.

Having ascertained that he was in full possession of

the agreed-upon sum, Dutta was all smiles. But his good spirits vanished when his aide returned alone.

"Where's the prisoner?" Dutta asked, frowning.

"She's in the infirmary," the aide replied.

"Why? Is she sick?"

"She's being examined by a doctor. For signs of cholera," the aide added.

"What doctor?" Dutta demanded. "Our man went home at nine o'clock."

"The doctor from the city health department's Disease Control Bureau. He just arrived."

"Oh, yes, now I remember," Dutta said. "The warden did mention something about a doctor coming tonight. But that prisoner isn't sick. She's a healthy specimen if ever I saw one."

The subordinate shrugged. "The doctor asked for her by name." Sensing the tension in the room, the aide quickly covered himself. "The warden told me to extend full cooperation to the doctor. I didn't think you wanted to be bothered with it."

Carter was already out of his chair. "Where's the infirmary?"

"In this wing," Dutta said.

"We'd better hurry," Carter said.

"You suspect foul play?"

"There might be if we don't move fast."

"One moment, please." Dutta unlocked the bottom drawer of the desk and took out a .44 magnum revolver with an eight-inch barrel. It was so big, it made the gun that Guptil had taken from Shaheed look like a child's toy.

When he saw the gun, the subordinate shifted into high gear. He dashed out of the office and rounded up some guards.

Deputy Warden Dutta came out from behind the desk, gun in hand, to lead the way. Guptil Gucharvi mentally kicked himself a dozen times over for handing over the cash before making sure that the "merchandise" was intact. No matter what happened to Vashti Takore, Deputy Warden Dutta would never give back the money.

Dutta, Carter, Guptil, Dutta's aide, and three guards charged down the long dim corridor. The guards didn't know what was going on, but when they saw Dutta's gun, they drew their own. Carter hoped like hell that nobody would get trigger-happy.

The running men rounded a corner and went down another, shorter hall. At its end lay the infirmary, its door closed. The door's upper half was made of translucent frosted glass, preventing them from seeing inside the room.

Dutta tried the doorknob. The door was locked.

"Break it open!" he shouted to the guards.

But he was so excited that he carried out the command himself. He smashed the gun barrel against the glass. The pane shattered but didn't break, further enraging Dutta.

From the other side of the door came a stifled cry.

A raging bull, Dutta swung again, wielding the gun like a club. That did it. The pane imploded, cascading crystal shards on the infirmary floor.

Dutta reached inside, unlocked the door, and kicked it open. But it was Nick Carter who went through the door first.

A bizarre tableau greeted him. A grotesquely fat nurse whose right foot was in a plaster cast wrestled with a female prisoner, holding her from behind. The beautiful prisoner was struggling with every ounce of strength, but she was helpless in the grip of the huge woman. A scrawny, sour-faced man in a white coat danced anxiously around the female combatants, holding a hypodermic syringe with his thumb poised on the plunger.

Carter didn't know who the enormous woman or the

man with the syringe was, but he was dead certain they had nothing to do with the city's Disease Control Bureau.

Primala—for indeed it was she in the nurse's uniform—had one hand clamped over the lower half of Vashti's face, pinching her nose shut and covering her mouth. Her other hand encircled Vashti's left wrist, holding her arm out, exposing the inner forearm for the man's needle.

Before swinging into action, Carter yelled in his limited Hindustani, "Don't shoot! You'll hit the girl!" Or himself. The last thing he wanted was to be caught in the middle if Dutta and the guards started blasting. He just hoped the guards understood his accent.

The scrawny man let go of the hypo and clawed for a gun in his pocket. He was still groping for it when Carter reached him. "Kill her!" the man shouted at the fat woman.

And then Carter was on him.

The man glimpsed a blur of slashing motion, Carter's open-handed strike. The edge of the Killmaster's hand chopped him across the throat.

At that instant, the man stopped being an active player in the game. He reeled backward, choking and gagging, crashing into a wall. He went down, unconscious.

Primala shifted tactics. The plan had been to knock out Vashti with a shot of a tranquilizing drug, load her on a gurney, and remove her from the prison on the pretext that she was highly infectious. Primala's masters wanted Vashti alive.

Since premature discovery had ruined that plan, Primala moved to exercise the second option, namely, killing Vashti. With her tremendous strength, Primala could snap a neck as easily as breaking a breadstick. She moved to do just that.

Vashti tried to kick Primala's bad foot, but the fat woman was ready for that. She hefted Vashti so her flailing feet were off the floor.

Vashti was nothing if not adaptable. Since she couldn't kick, she did the next best thing. She sank her teeth into the hand that Primala held over her mouth and bit down on the fingers as hard as she could, grinding her teeth into the bones.

Carter reached the struggling women, the huge one now shrieking in pain. He grabbed Primala's arm to apply a punishing submission hold. The restraint technique called for him to bend her arm behind her back, then to apply maximum leverage. But no matter how much force he exerted, he couldn't budge her arm. The woman was built like an ox, and her agony didn't diminish her strength.

The Killmaster knew how to counter brute force, however. He moved behind Primala and unleashed a powerful right to the back of her head. His fist crashed into her occipital bulge, that nerve nexus where the back of the skull joins the neck. It was a devastating strike, one which could knock out or even kill an opponent when properly applied.

This strike was properly applied. There was a harsh popping sound when his knuckles connected. Primala was staggered, but she wasn't out.

Still, the blow forced her to release Vashti. Vashti loosened her bulldog grip on the hand she was biting, and slipped free, running to the other side of the room.

Primala turned, confronting Carter. He was amazed; this crazed fat woman was a force of nature. He'd hit her with a blow that would have finished most men, but she was coming back for more.

Dutta yelled at his men. "Don't just stand there, you morons! Stop that woman!"

The guards brought their nightsticks into play, clubbing Primala from behind. While she was fighting them off, Carter took the opportunity to get past her.

Primala's injured foot handicapped her. She started to go down under a rain of bludgeoning blows. A guard moved in, nightstick raised, to deliver the knockout. Primala grabbed his arm, pulling him forward. The guard hollered as his feet left the floor. Primala got her football-player shoulders under his middle, then unbent her legs.

Suddenly the guard was slung over her back and being whirled around in a breathless airplane spin. The foot in a cast, the bitten, bleeding hand, the damaging blows she had already sustained—all of these were shrugged off by Primala, who was now in a berserk rage.

The whirling guard's foot hit Dutta's aide in the jaw, and the man was slammed backward into an instrument cart. He fell on top of it, clearing it of instruments, bottles, vials, and other medical paraphernalia. The wheeled cart zoomed across the room, unwillingly ridden by Dutta's semiconscious subordinate.

The guard who still had both feet on the floor tried a new tactic. Instead of clubbing with the nightstick, he held it in both hands and thrust it at Primala. A promising idea and one that might have proved effective if Primala hadn't thrown the other guard at him. The two went down in a groaning tangle of arms and legs, looking like some exotic multilimbed Hindu deity.

For a moment Primala appeared victorious, then Deputy Warden Dutta's gun barrel slammed the back of her skull. Dutta had managed to get behind her while she was occupied with the others. She reeled, eyes going in and out of focus. Dutta took no chances. He hit her a second time, harder, and Primala hit the floor with a thud that shook the building. Dutta was most pleased with himself, but not so happy that he lost sight of the now conscious "doctor" crawling on hands and knees toward the door.

Vashti was edging that way herself, when Nick Carter took hold of her elbow. Vashti turned—and looked up at AXE's finest. She liked what she saw. The stranger had a slightly battered but still handsome face, and though he held her firmly without hurting her, there was something hard in his eyes, a hint of cruelty and more than a touch of danger. And then Nick Carter smiled at her, and Vashti had second thoughts about escaping.

Eyelashes fluttering, lips parted, Vashti slumped into a faint—or she pretended to. She was caught up in a pair of strong arms, one cradling her back, the other under her knees. She sighed, resting her head against his chest.

Guptil grinned. The Carter charm never failed; even in the most unlikely circumstances.

Meanwhile, Deputy Warden Dutta had halted the scrawny man's progress toward the door with a gun muzzle pressed to the back of his head.

A new group of guards stampeded into view.

"Do not worry," Deputy Warden Dutta announced. "Everything is under control!"

Groaning, Primala squirmed on the floor, trying to rise from her prone position.

"Arrest that woman!" Dutta commanded. "Put her in irons, and don't take any chances! Make them double strength!"

The guard who had been knocked down by the other guard shook his head to clear it. He warned the reinforcements, "Be careful! She's as strong as a buffalo!"

Primala vanished from view as she was encircled by guards, all of whom were competing to demonstrate their zeal.

Somebody lent a hand to the guard who'd gone for an airplane ride on Primala's back. His complexion was a pasty yellow. He wobbled to the sink and vomited.

Helping hands assisted Dutta's aide. A huge bruise mottled his jaw where he had been kicked. "My jaw," he croaked, his voice garbled. "I think it's broken."

"What should we do with him?" a guard asked Dutta.

"Take him to the infirmary," Dutta started to say, when he realized that they were in the infirmary. The place was a shambles. "Take him to my office. We'll send for a doctor."

The sour-faced man crouched on the floor on his hands and knees said, "I'm a doctor."

Dutta snickered. "Of course you are. Now, suppose you tell me who you are and what your little game is."

The man clammed up.

"Oh, so you won't talk, eh?" Dutta said. "We'll see if we can convince you to be a bit more forthcoming!"

"You'd better check with your boss before you do anything you'll regret," the man in the doctor's coat snapped.

"What's that supposed to mean?"

"It means you'd better have a little talk with the warden," the scrawny man said. "That's all I'm going to say."

"Throw him in a cell!" Dutta ordered. "But, er, don't do anything else until you hear from me."

"Yes, sir," a guard said.

Carter was beginning to tire of holding Vashti, and started to put her down.

Vashti surprised him by asking in English, "Don't you like holding me?"

"At any other time it would be a pleasure," Carter said. "But this is business. You want to get out of here, don't you?"

Indeed she did. Carter set her down. While disengaging herself, Vashti managed to rub against his well-muscled torso. The curve of her hip grazed his groin. Carter felt the subtle movement, but hid his smile.

The group of guards groaned under the strain of haul-

ing Primala to her feet. She and her partner were
dragged away to be locked up.

Dutta had been silent and thoughtful ever since the
phony doctor made that crack about checking with the
warden. The Killmaster didn't want him thinking too
hard.

"Congratulations, Deputy!" Carter said. "You'll be
a hero when the word gets out about how you single-
handedly captured this gang."

"But who are they?" Dutta asked.

Carter pitched his voice low, so only Dutta could hear
it. "If I may ask you a personal question, Deputy, did
either of those characters make any, er, financial arrangements with you?"

"They most certainly did not!"

"In other words, they tried to embarrass you by
carrying away one of your charges without even having
the decency to renumerate you, the way I did."

"The swine!" Dutta's outrage was genuine. The very
idea that a private deal had gone down in the prison
without him being cut in for a piece of the action was
truly infuriating.

Carter continued. "Won't the warden be surprised
when he discovers that you caught the gang in the act
and have them under lock and key?"

"I'll say he will!"

"You'll be a hero. You might even be in line for a
promotion."

"The only job above mine is the warden's," Dutta
said.

"Need I say more?" Carter smiled, then answered his
own question. "Oh, yes, there is something else. The
ambulance outside has two men in it. Unless I miss my
guess, they're in on this plan. If you act fast, you can
make a clean sweep of them!"

"I'll show them!" Dutta vowed through clenched

teeth. "The swine!" he shouted again, and stormed off.

Carter took Vashti's hand and followed him. Not only was he not going to let her out of his sight, he wasn't going to let her out of his reach. He didn't know what she'd seen, but he'd almost lost her, and he wasn't going to let it happen again.

Dutta delegated a guard to round up more of his colleagues. The deputy warden unlocked an oversize wooden wall cabinet in the warden's office. It was filled with weapons, rifles, shotguns, and plenty of ammunition. More guards showed up and Dutta handed out the weapons to them. Then he reached way into the back of the cabinet and hauled out his personal best, a submachine gun. He slapped a hundred-round drum into the receiver.

A guard was on the telephone, passing the word to the gate and tower guards. He hung up, reporting, "They're ready and waiting for you to give the signal, sir!"

"I'll give the signal, all right," Dutta muttered. "Follow me, men!"

"Okay if we tag along for the show?" Carter said.

"Just don't get in the way."

"We won't," Carter said solemnly.

The crushing night heat was forgotten in the excitement. Dutta led the pack, cradling his submachine gun, jogging down the halls, his legs pumping like pistons. The squad of guards trotted after him, hustling to keep up.

Carter, Vashti, and Guptil followed well to the rear. Carter didn't plan to get in front of that local version of the Keystone Kops, not with all the firepower they were packing so casually and carelessly. He still had hold of Vashti's hand and she didn't seem to object.

Even the normally phlegmatic Guptil was caught up in the excitement. "What a night! What a night!"

"Yeah, and it's not over yet," Carter reminded him.

The two men in the ambulance were smoking and trying to stay awake when Deputy Warden Dutta and his troops stormed out the door and ranked themselves into a firing line spanning the width of the courtyard. Up on the twin towers, powerful searchlights came to life, lighting the courtyard like a movie set.

Dutta didn't need a bull horn. He bellowed, "Come out with your hands up!" At the same time, he engaged his weapon and threw off the safety.

The ambulance driver put the vehicle into gear and floored the gas pedal. The ambulance was parked facing the prison. The driver threw it into reverse, figuring he would blow the vehicle rear-first into the gate and crash through.

He never made it.

Dutta didn't order his men to commence firing. He pulled the trigger of his submachine gun, squeezing off a long burst. His men picked up their cue and cut loose.

Carter, Vashti, and Guptil took cover inside the prison door. Vashti huddled against Carter, saying, "I'm so frightened! Please hold me!"

Carter didn't completely believe her, but he held her close anyway.

Tires squealing, the ambulance zoomed backward, fishtailing crazily. The prison guards weren't the best shots in the world, but it was tough to miss the target in that closed courtyard. The ambulance was peppered with scores of slugs.

The submachine gun had a hell of a kick, but that didn't stop the deputy warden. Dutta stood braced with his legs spread wide, fighting his weapon's jackhammer recoil as it pumped bullets.

The men in the ambulance were probably already dead, but the vehicle kept going backward until it slammed into the gate. The rear of the ambulance crumpled like an accordion, but the iron grillwork held.

Dutta kept pouring slugs into the ambulance, and the guards followed his example. Dutta devoutly wished that it was the warden he was gunning down. A fellow can get awfully sick of being the second banana, the number two man, especially when his boss cuts him out of the gravy deals.

The fire reached the gas tank. The ambulance exploded, engulfed in a white-hot fireball.

"What a night! What a night!" Guptil kept exclaiming.

Carter had some advice for him. "Next time, don't mess around with any assistants. Buy the boss."

FIVE

Six hours and 459 miles later, Carter had Vashti Takore stashed away in a safe house in a New Delhi suburb. The cover story handed out to the locals was that the facility was maintained by one of the big, multinational conglomerates for the use of visiting high-level executives. Actually, it belonged to AXE and was run under the direction of veteran operative Pete Barnes.

The CIA had extensive facilities similar to this one in the area, but Carter was steering clear of them. The Company had lost an entire sub-branch of its network when their men had disappeared. With ruthless logic, Carter had to proceed on the assumption that the cover was blown on every one of their safe houses, field agents, contacts, and covert operatives.

Carter was in a second-floor bedroom. Vashti was in

the adjoining bathroom, freshening up. Guptil Gucharvi was busy chasing around town, trying to cut a deal to spring the rest of the Takore clan from the local authorities. Pete Barnes was downstairs in the security cockpit, manning the control console that was the brain of the sophisticated electronics gear monitoring the safe house compound, the eight-foot-high wall surrounding it, and all avenues of approach.

The compound had its own generator that protected its security surveillance equipment from being blinded by a power outage. The safe house had air conditioning. The air conditioners were roaring at full blast and the indoor temperature was in the mid-eighties. Considering that it was thirty degrees hotter outside and getting worse, that wasn't too bad.

Carter peeled off his jacket. It was soaked with sweat. He doubted that the best dry cleaner in the world would be able to bring it back to life. He draped it on a hanger, hung it from a door frame, then walked to a comfortable chair and sat down, his thoughts now on Wilhelmina. The 9mm Luger under his arm was a collector's item classic of pre-WW II vintage. Carter periodically had the weapon retooled by a seventy-year-old German-American gunsmith from Milwaukee, a master craftsman of the art, a wizard, a maestro. And the AXE technicians repaired her when necessary. As a result, Wilhelmina was in better shape today than she was when she was first made.

Carter shucked the pistol clear of its holster, noting that the soggy leather didn't want to let go of the gun. That could slow up his draw enough to get him killed.

He held Wilhelmina up, examining the weapon. Was that some trick of the light, or were there some new scratches dulling the blued finish? He couldn't tell for sure. The curtains were drawn, the room was dim, and he wasn't going to turn on any lamps. That would only make the damned place hotter, he thought tiredly.

The cleanliness of the safe house was a joy, the relative coolness of the air conditioning sheer heaven. But the sight of the big pink bathtub held the greatest pleasure for ex-prisoner Vashti Takore.

Vashti cracked open the bathroom door, peeked through the opening, and saw Carter sitting in an armchair by the window, fiddling with his gun. She eased the door shut, making sure that it wasn't locked. And then, since she was a *malka-sansi*, and her business was theft, she inspected the bathroom's sole window.

Mounted high on the wall, it was a long thin rectangle of thick glass set in a steel frame. Inside the glass was a grid of fine silver wires, delicate as a cat's whiskers. Like all the rest of the window glass in the house, this glass was shatter-resistant and bulletproof. And if somebody somehow managed to break the glass, those hair-fine sensor wires would trigger a red alert on the control console.

When Vashti saw that she couldn't get out of the window, she put it out of her mind. Even if she could, she didn't think she'd leave just yet. There was plenty in the safe house to enjoy as long as she was here. She thought of the man seated in the adjoining room and smiled.

The thought of Carter reminded her that she had some cleaning up to do; she wanted to make herself as attractive, as seductive as possible.

She peeled out of her filthy prison garb, her flesh shrinking from the coarse fabric. After stripping them off, the very idea that she had worn those rags for three days made her shudder. Holding them at arm's length, she dropped them into the wastebasket under the sink. She hoped that somebody would take them out and burn them.

After her prison stay, the immaculate bathroom seemed as luxurious as a maharajah's palace. Vashti delighted in the light, the space, the tile and porcelain, the gleaming stainless-steel fixtures, the wall of mirrors.

First on the agenda was to scrub the prison stink and filth from her pores. She turned on the shower as hot and hard as she could stand it. Standing under the steaming spray, she used a big loofah to scour herself all over. She didn't stop until her skin was tinged with pink. Her whole body tingled and she felt wonderful.

When she was done with the shower, she filled the tub with hot water. The safe house often had female guests, so there was a variety of bath salts, body oils, creams, lotions, and moisturizers on the shelves. Even scented bubble bath, which Vashti poured into the tub.

The shower was cleansing, but the bath was a sensual experience. Sighing happily, Vashti lowered herself into the tub and soaked. She lay there with her eyes closed and wondered what she would do next.

After a while she had an idea and giggled to herself. Mountains of soap bubbles floated on top of the water. Vashti gathered a double armload to her, pressing the stuff to her body to conceal her breasts. She lifted a shapely leg out of the tub and pushed the door open with her foot.

"Nick . . . ?"

It hadn't taken them long to get on a first-name basis. Carter came over and stood in the doorway.

"Would you please wash my back?"

"Sure."

Carter stripped off his shoulder holster and hung it on the doorknob.

"I know what you are," Vashti said.

"What am I?"

"A gangster," Vashti said.

"Thanks a lot," Carter said, amused. "What makes you say that?"

"That gun. That knife on your arm."

"What, this old thing?" Carter said dryly. He undid the thin straps of the spring-loaded chamois sheath from his forearm. Nestled inside it was Hugo, his razor-sharp stiletto. A twist of the wrist would trip the spring catch and propel the knife hilt-first into his right hand.

"Wouldn't want to get this wet." Carter carefully put Hugo aside—within his reach, but not within Vashti's. She was a variable factor in the equation, an unknown quantity. Carter was cautious; it went with the territory.

"I'm sure you're a gangster," Vashti stated. "You're armed and dangerous. You don't act like a government man, and you're too good-looking to be a policeman."

"And you're too beautiful to be a thief."

"But I am a thief." Some of her soap bubbles floated away, baring a dark brown nipple. Vashti didn't bother to cover it. "I am a thief, and you are a . . . what? How do you call it? Oh, yes. A hit man. You're a hit man, aren't you?"

"You could say that."

"You're not joking." Vashti was touched with a chill, a shiver that ran along her spine, a frisson that was far from unpleasant. "You're serious. You mean it. You—what are you doing?"

Carter peeled off his soggy shirt. He was already barefoot. He took off his pants.

"Now, just a minute—" Vashti said.

Carter took off his undershorts. Vashti looked at him, stared at him, her eyes taking in the scarred, powerful body. Smiling, Carter climbed into the tub and sat down behind her. She sat between his legs with her back to him.

"You said you wanted your back washed. I'll get around to that. Later." Carter reached forward, encircling her with his arms. She was wet and sleek and smooth. Heat suffused her skin.

Carter found a washcloth and a bar of soap. He

lathered up Vashti's firm breasts, caressing them very gently. His fingers ran lightly over her hard nipples.

"Ummmmm," Vashti sighed. She could feel his body moving slowly against her back. She wriggled with pleasure.

Carter chuckled. "Glad you're enjoying it." He stuck his head over her shoulder and nibbled her ear. He was so distracted by what he was doing that somehow he managed to drop the soap. It fell between Vashti's thighs.

"I'll get it," Carter said. His fingers found more than the soap, and he knew all the right places and all the right ways to touch her.

Vashti felt as if she were dissolving in the hot water. Surely there was a fire under the tub, bringing it to a boil. Her head tilted back, her eyes were half-closed, her lips parted.

Then the magic fingers went away. "Don't stop," she moaned softly.

"I won't." Carter's hands were on her, guiding, stroking, urging, arousing.

Water and foam sloshed in the tub as Vashti changed positions. She turned around so she knelt facing him. Carter thought she was a splendid creature, with the muscle tone of an athlete and the physique of a temple dancer. She knelt with her folded legs on either side of him. Under satin skin, bands of muscle flexed in her shapely, quivering thighs. Where those thighs joined, she was as soft as a flower.

Carter placed his hands on her wide hips, pulling her closer to him. She put her hands on his thighs and slid herself up to his groin.

Her breasts bobbed in front of Carter's face. He pressed his lips against them. They were wet and sleek and perfect. Carter put one of her dark nipples in his mouth and sucked it. Soon he gave the other equal time.

When he could stand it no longer, Carter leaned back and guided Vashti's hips over his. She lowered herself onto him, and with a powerful thrust he entered her. She adjusted her hips, squirming as the full length of him penetrated her. She was all molten heat inside.

Carter moved, clenched buttocks sliding against the tub, legs bent, hands holding Vashti's hips. He thrust into her again and again. Their writhing bodies created tidal waves of bathwater that splashed over the side of the tub. Excitement soared to its ecstatic peak and then somehow went beyond it. Carter's pleasure centers were hit with a current of high-voltage sparks that blew their needles right off the dials.

Then Vashti cried out and everything was a blur. . . .

Pete Barnes had a top-priority communication coming in on the satellite beam. The transmission emanated from a phone at AXE headquarters on Dupont Circle in Washington, D.C. Automatically encrypted and scrambled, the signal was beamed up to a geosynchronous communications satellite orbiting at an altitude of 23,000 miles. The signal was beamed down to a receiving station on the other side of the planet. It was switched through various channels, received by the communications console in Pete Barnes's New Delhi safe house, decoded, and unscrambled.

And it was all done in real time, permitting AXE's director to conduct a conversation with a party on the other side of the world.

But it takes two to talk, and the party to whom the director wanted to speak was currently unavailable. Pete Barnes was forced to put his boss, the irascible David Hawk, on hold.

Barnes was only stepping out of the security center for as long as it took to race upstairs and inform Nick Carter that he was wanted on the phone, but he paused to lock the door and rattle the knob to make sure it was locked. A man develops certain habits and reflexes after working for AXE for over two decades. They save lives.

The door to the bedroom suite was closed. Barnes raised his hand to knock on it when he heard a woman's shriek. Instinctively, he flung open the door, bursting into the bedroom. It was unoccupied. The bathroom door was open and another cry pierced the air.

Wishing he'd brought a gun, Barnes hurried to the bathroom. He looked inside, then let out his breath.

"Uh, Nick . . . ?" Abashed, Barnes discreetly averted his gaze.

Carter looked toward the doorway and focused his eyes. "Yeah?"

Still not looking, Barnes mumbled, "Message from D.C. The boss wants to talk to you."

"Shit." Carter cleared the fuzz from his brain and looked at Vashti poised above him. Then he looked at Barnes. "Tell Hawk I'll call him back. Now that the lady and I have gotten acquainted, we have some talking to do."

"But—" Barnes began.

"Don't worry. Just go, and tell him I'll be talking to him shortly. He'll probably yell a bit, but it'll be me he's mad at, not you. Thanks, Pete—now scram! See you later."

Shaking his head, not looking forward to Hawk's reaction, Barnes hurried from the bedroom suite.

Carter grabbed some towels from a nearby rack and handed them to a disappointed Vashti.

"All good things must come to an end, I fear. Wrap yourself up in these and meet me in the bedroom. There are some things I have to know. For starters, suppose you tell me why a *malka-sansi* from Delhi is suddenly at the top of everybody's hit parade."

It turned out to be quite a story.

SIX

Not unlike a spy, a successful thief needs a network of reliable informants. An ambitious and hungry band like the Takores had a particularly extensive backfield of scouts always on the lookout for lucrative prospects. Each member of the family had his or her own string of spotters.

Narayan Takore had come to his sister Vashti with some confidential information. They were a year apart in age and had shared many interests while growing up; this forged a close bond that had persisted to the present day.

Like most Indian families, the Takore clan was very much a patriarchy. The father was long dead, so leadership rested on the shoulders of the eldest son, Sanjay. Since Vashti and Narayan were junior members, their words carried little weight in family councils. Adding to their inferior status was the fact that Vashti was a woman and that Narayan was perceived as a lazy good-for-nothing drunk. When the time came for dividing the loot from a job, they received the smallest shares, no matter how great their contribution to the group enterprise.

So Narayan came to Vashti with an interesting business proposition. One of his spotters had discovered a promising prospect for plunder. Narayan suggested that he and Vashti do the job themselves, without informing the rest of the family. That way, they could divide the take straight down the middle and not see the lion's share grabbed by their elders.

Narayan was a competent thief when sober, which wasn't often. But he was clumsy and earthbound compared to Vashti, who was a cat burglar *par excellence*.

Before the job was pulled, extensive groundwork would be required. The premises would have to be scouted for security, entrances, exits, avenues of approach and escape, number of personnel, and all the other details that spell the difference between success and failure.

Vashti agreed to inspect the site. If it panned out, she and her brother would pull the job. She entered into the agreement with misgivings, since her affection for Narayan did not blind her to his frequent unreliability.

Her qualms increased on the night picked for casing the site. Narayan, who was supposed to serve as her lookout, was drunk. Vashti was disgusted, but she was determined to do her part. Her personal reserves of cash were running low and she would work without Narayan. No lookout was better than a drunk one.

The early morning hours found her prowling an unfamiliar district of Old Delhi. Despite the heat, she was shrouded in a dark sari and veil, hidden in its voluminous folds. She shuffled forward, affecting the gait and mannerisms of an old woman as she examined the address supplied by Narayan's spotter.

Bounded by a polluted tributary of the Jumna River, the neighborhood was a crazy-quilt patchwork that alternated blocks of teeming slums, crumbling ruins, and once proud but now run-down residential sections.

The targeted site sat on the west bank of the nameless river, once upon a time prime real estate for the British merchant princes of the East India Company. Wealthy but homesick for England, they commissioned their architects to build majestic town houses and mansions that would re-create a bit of London in the heart of the raj.

Since then, the square had declined as much as the empire. Neglect and decay blanketed crumbling piles of masonry, some of them so unsafe that even the squatters shunned them. Gaps yawned in the rows of houses. Rubble-strewn lots were given over to weeds, rats, and the bold packs of jackals unafraid to roam streets only a few miles distant from the nation's capital.

But one house in particular was distinguished by curious comings and goings. This was the house that Vashti watched.

The building and its grounds must have been beautiful a century earlier, Vashti thought. The main structure was a sprawling four-story red brick mansion constructed late enough in the Victorian period to boast extravagant ornamentation.

Its grounds and outbuildings occupied an entire block. Its front faced west. Its rear was turned to the river, where steep stone stairs spilled down to a landing on the water. Its south face fronted a narrow lane that stood at right angles to the river. On the other side of the lane was a gutted, burnt-out church. Its north face looked out onto a vacant lot.

The house was set well back from the square and was bounded by a brick wall ten feet high. The main gate was set in the middle of the west wall. A small door stood in the south wall. The east wall had an opening allowing access to the river landing.

Inside the walls, the grounds provided plenty of places to hide because of the piles of rubble covering the area. The place showed every sign of having been abandoned for decades. But it had new tenants now.

The main gate was manned by armed guards. During Vashti's vigil, they opened the gate to allow expensive automobiles to enter, luxury cars that jarred with the scene of almost bombed-out desolation. Once through the gates, the cars followed the horseshoe-shaped drive leading to the main entrance, a columned portico topped by a triangular pediment. The cars discharged their passengers—well-dressed men and a few women —who disappeared inside the building.

In the space of an hour, Vashti counted some fourteen persons going inside.

Who were they? What were they doing there?

Her guess was that it was something illegal. Gambling, drugs, prostitution—perhaps all three. That was good. Vice meant money. Narayan's spotter might have unearthed a likely prospect after all. Further investigation was warranted.

Vashti planned her approach carefully, after long perusal of the scene. An hour passed; no more cars arrived. Vashti made her move.

Gaining entry to the grounds was easy. She worked her way along the riverbank to the landing, climbed to the top, and slipped shadowlike through the gap in the wall.

Behind the cover of a pile of rubble, she shrugged out of the dark sari. Beneath it she wore her working clothes: black T-shirt, black slacks, black sneakers. Her hair was pulled back into a single long braid. She wore an ornate copper ring at the braid's end, not for ornamentation, but because its weight made her aware of its position, aiding her balance. A long length of thin nylon rope was knotted around her middle.

Taking advantage of the available cover, she zigzagged her way to the rear of the mansion. A quick, thorough survey showed that there was no way she could enter from the ground floor. She would not risk an approach from any other side of the building, since she could be seen by the gate guards.

No glass remained in the windows. All the windows on the ground floor had been boarded up. Red light filtered through gaps in the boards, but she was unable to see what was going on inside. Voices rose and fell, but individual words were impossible to make out.

Her practiced eye quickly found a way to get in. It went straight up.

A balcony jutted out on the second floor, facing the river. The room beyond it was dark, seemingly empty, and barred only by a few haphazardly placed planks. The balcony balustrade was studded with various protruding knobs and decorative curlicues carved in the stone.

Vashti uncoiled her rope, fixing a loop at one end. After a number of unsuccessful casts, she threw the loop around one of the balcony's projecting knobs. She tested it with her weight. It held.

Up she went, twenty feet from the ground, using the building's decorative bands of ornamental stonework for footholds. Still, it was no easy climb. When she finally set foot on the balcony, she coiled the rope so it would not be seen by anyone at ground level and left it tied to the balcony rail for a quick getaway.

The night was dark—there was no moon—but Vashti had good night vision. The inner room was black except for the thinnest, faintest glow on the wall opposite the balcony. Vashti guessed that it was light shining under a door.

A few old planks were nailed diagonally across the

balcony entrance. Vashti ducked under the lowest and squeezed through into the room. Grit scratched underfoot. Vashti walked on the outer edges of her shoes to minimize the sound of her footsteps.

In the darkness, like a bat, she used her other senses to compensate for her inability to really see anything. Every square inch of her skin was a sensing device, monitoring minute changes in air pressure and currents. Her ears were the next best thing to sonar.

They warned her that she was not alone.

She was about halfway to the bit of light peeking under the door when she made that dismaying discovery. She froze. The room was as dark as a tomb, and Vashti did not want it to be her final resting place.

A low moan nearly made her jump out of her skin. The sound was repeated. She couldn't tell if it had been made by an animal or a man. A choked, muffled gargle, half sob, half groan. Her arms were covered with gooseflesh as she stood there listening.

The mournful cry was enough for her. She would make her exit, and fast. Turning to back out, she stumbled into something. Something big, moist, and fleshy, something alive that groaned at her touch.

She couldn't suppress a cry, and immediately clapped her hand over her mouth, cursing herself. How could she be so stupid as to cry out?

Her touch sparked a frenzied outburst from the moaner. Raw, formless cries came from it, rising into ragged frenzy. It sounded like a mute having an epileptic fit.

But what was worse, the moans summoned others.

From beyond the door came querulous voices and pounding footsteps, and they were approaching quickly.

Vashti raced to the balcony and wriggled under the boards. Once outside, she stood flat against the wall.

She was afraid to make a break for it. She knew that staying put is often more effective than taking it on the run. Breathless, heart hammering, Vashti prayed they wouldn't decide to look on the balcony.

Inside, the darkness ebbed under the tide of gray light pouring in through the open door.

The steady groaning peaked in a crescendo of fear.

A blow was struck.

The moans subsided into dull whimperings.

"That's better," a man said. "I've had enough of your noise."

A second man said, laughing, "Don't worry, Sundram, you won't have to put up with it for much longer. This dog has reached the end of his leash."

Vashti was satisfied that her presence was unsuspected by the newcomers. She realized that her curiosity might jeopardize her safety, but she just had to peek inside that room.

What she saw made her blood run cold.

The moaner was a man. He was tied naked to a high-backed wooden armchair. What struck Vashti first was that he was a Westerner, with longish silver-gray hair and dark bushy sideburns. He was pale, shriveled, wrinkled as an elephant's knee, and his skin was almost as gray.

He was bound to the chair with strands of barbed wire. Surgical tape was pasted across his mouth, which explained his throaty moans. The man had obviously been tortured.

The other two men were Indian. One was bearded and wore a traditional high-necked tunic and loose white cotton breeches. The other was smaller, clean-shaven, and wore a sport shirt and jeans.

The bearded man grabbed a handful of the prisoner's shaggy hair and yanked his head back. The silver-haired man groaned. The Indian then let go of his head, which fell forward, chin slumped on chest.

The bearded man chuckled. "A tough old bird, this one. But in the end, he talked. They all do."

"He was never in danger of dying, Bharat," the other Indian said. "Not from the questioning."

"No, Sundram, he's destined for better things," Bharat said. "And I hope soon. He's already starting to stink and he's not even dead yet!"

More voices sounded in the hall. Sundram stuck his head out the door to take a look. "Looks like you'll get your wish, Bharat," he reported. "Here they come."

Bharat flexed his fingers. "I'd just as soon finish both those foreign dogs, too," he muttered.

Sundram laughed. "Restrain yourself, my impetuous friend. Personally, I hope our generous patrons live long lives—at least while they remain our paymasters."

Three men entered the room.

The first was a burly, hawk-faced, bearded Indian whom the others addressed as Turan. Despite his beautiful clothes, he had the aspect of a gutter-tough hoodlum—and the gutters of India's big cities are as tough as they come. Sundram and Bharat deferred to Turan, who exercised some authority over them—whether by rank or by virtue of his superior ferocity, Vashti could not tell.

Trailing Turan were two Westerners. The smaller of the pair was a medium-sized man with sandy hair and a narrow, skeletal face. He was thin and reedy, his complexion sallow under a deep tan. His eyes were the most animated part of him, hot cinders set deep in hollow sockets.

He went over to the prisoner and patted him on the head. "Hullo, Granger, old sport."

"The goddess grows impatient," Turan said. "The Gopalaswami wants to know when we can have this man."

"Now," the other member of the foreign duo said. "We're done with him."

This man had a striking, almost theatrical appearance. He was fiftyish, big and broad-shouldered, and his powerful body was clad in a white silk suit that even the terrible heat had not wilted. He had a full head of wavy salt-and-pepper hair and a neatly trimmed Vandyke to match.

"Take off his gag, Lundy," he ordered.

The bony-faced man snapped, in a voice whose accent betrayed his English origin, "Why don't you do it yourself?"

"Because I don't want to get my hands dirty."

"Well, I like that! What about my hands—"

"And because I'm paying."

"All right, all right," Lundy grumbled. "I suppose it won't do me any harm to oblige a friend."

Lundy worked on Granger's gag. The adhesive was powerful and he had to work in close. His pointed nose crinkled in disgust. "God, he smells!"

Lundy finally pulled off the gag, then fastidiously wiped his fingers on a handkerchief. His partner poked the semiconscious prisoner to get his attention.

After a series of sharp jabs, Granger responded. He lacked the strength to lift his chin from his chest, but he had just enough left to look up at his tormentor with eyes of hate.

The smirking white-suited man had spoken to Turan in Hindustani, as had Lundy. He now spoke to Granger in English. As it was for so many in India, English was a second language for all the Takores, so Vashti was able to follow the exchange.

"This is it, Granger," the white-suited man said. "You're the last of them."

Lundy laughed. "That's right, we saved the best for last."

"Now it's your turn. Any last words, Granger?"

"Yeah," Granger croaked. "Fuck you, Rogov."

At this point, Nick Carter interrupted Vashti's recitation. "Hold on. What name did you just say?"

"Rogov," Vashti repeated. "That's what it sounded like to me. Yes, I'm sure it was Rogov."

Something came into Carter's face, something so cold and hard and pitiless that Vashti suddenly realized that when all was said and done, she had indeed lavished her caresses on a killer. She'd guessed correctly.

"You know him, don't you," she said softly. "Rogov, I mean."

"Yeah," Carter said, almost to himself. "I know him."

SEVEN

"Are you finished with him? Quite finished?" Turan asked.

"Oh, quite," Lundy replied. "You can have him with our compliments."

A wooden table stood against the wall. A variety of tools lay on it. Turan picked up a pair of wire cutters. The dark red stains on the blades were not rust. He started toward the man in the chair.

Terror gave Granger the strength to recoil from Turan. "No . . . no, don't! For God's sake, don't!"

Lundy turned to Rogov. "We don't have to watch this, do we?"

"You'll excuse us," Rogov said. "My partner has a weak stomach."

Turan chuckled. "This time the only thing I'm going to cut are these strands."

The barbed wire binding Granger's ankles and wrists to the chair parted with springing sounds when the cutter clipped them.

"You are welcome to join us in our worship," Turan said.

"Thanks awfully," Lundy drawled, "but we'll be running along now. We just wanted to say our good-byes to our chum."

"As you wish," Turan said, then turned to his men. "Bring him!"

Sundram and Bharat got on either side of the feebly protesting Granger. They each grabbed an arm and hauled him out of the chair.

Vashti saw a sadistic refinement when Granger was yanked to his feet. The chair's seat had been removed, no doubt to allow the torturers free and easy access to the victim's genitals.

Then her attention was diverted to more immediate concerns. Outside, voices approached. She did her best to blend into the shadows. She crouched in a corner of the balcony, looking down through spaces in its elaborately carved railings.

Two guards strolled down the path, chatting. They went to the top of the stone stairs leading down to the river and took a look around. They showed no signs of alarm, so Vashti guessed they were only making their regular rounds. One of the guards went to the side of the path and urinated in the bushes. Both guards then lit up cigarettes and stood there laughing and talking, showing no inclination to move on.

Vashti looked back into the room. It was vacant. Silent. What sort of house of horrors had she stumbled across? she wondered. Curiosity nagged her. She had to know. A reward might well be forthcoming for the person who denounced this band of brigands to the police. Vashti would never inform on any of the city's native criminal gangs, but this bunch was unknown to her.

Unable to resist the challenge, she slipped back into the room. Silence assured her that the men had deserted this area of the house. As she edged her way to the door, her gaze was drawn to the instruments of torture piled on the table. She shuddered at the grisly display.

The hall was empty. Taking a deep breath, Vashti began to tiptoe down its length, wishing she had a gun or even her trusty tiger claws.

Smoky red light flickered at the end of the hallway. There was a faint sweet smell of incense and some rustling noises.

Three stone steps, a turning, then three more stone steps brought her to a gallery overlooking the house's central great hall. Stout iron chains hung from the roof beams. At their ends dangled red-paned, wrought-iron lanterns that bathed the space with a hellish glow.

The U-shaped gallery stood about twenty feet above the ground floor. It hugged three walls, and an ornate, waist-high balustrade ran all along its length. Spaced along it at regular intervals were stone pillars supporting the arches of the roof.

Vashti dropped to her belly, slithered to the rail, and took a look.

The hall was a temple and its occupants were performing a simple religious ceremony. Of the two dozen worshippers gathered below, all but a handful were male. The people came from all walks of life. Some wore plain cotton shifts and loose trousers; others were smartly attired in European business suits. Their ages ranged from the very young to the very old, but the majority were middle-aged.

The altar stood against the wall that the gallery failed to span. A life-size statue of a goddess stood on a raised dais. It was a representation of a beautiful young female, nearly nude, whose voluptuous charms and sinuous grace were not unlike those of Vashti herself, and was posed in an attitude of graceful abandon.

The statue was made of gold. Her eyes were walnut-size blood rubies. Strands of milky pearls bedecked her shoulders. Her limbs were adorned with circlets of fresh flowers. Incense streamed from brass pots at her feet.

She was the goddess Kali and this place was a *kalighat*, a temple devoted to her worship.

The statue depicted her in her incarnation as the lovely bride of Siva, eminently desirable. Behind the statue, a tapestry covering the wall depicted Kali in yet another of her multiform aspects.

With its lurid, glowing colors, the tapestry was a window into hell. Only the hell it depicted was this world, not the next. It was a world on fire, where swarming hordes of armies clashed in titanic slaughter. Bestriding this war world like a colossus was the grotesque figure of a hag, stringy-haired and purple-skinned, reveling in chaos and death. She, too, was Kali, in her incarnation as the Dark Mother, the Goddess of Death.

Kali was worshipped by millions of law-abiding citizens in India, but the sect associated with this temple was something altogether different. They were members of the age-old cult of Thuggee, the infamous Thugs.

A high priest stood with his back to the statue as he faced Granger and the band of believers. Granger crouched on the floor, legs folded under him, hands tied behind his back.

The Thugs were chanting: "*Kali mayi ki jai!*"—Long live the goddess Kali!

This was their ritual mantra. Constant repetition of the words of power put them in a suggestible, even hypnotic state.

The priest signaled for the ceremony to begin. Three men stepped forward, Turan and two others. Turan took up the *ruhmal*, the sacred golden strangling cord of the Thugs.

Kali created the Thugs to destroy demons, or so went the legend. If the demons' blood was spilled, each drop would become a new demon. The killings had to be done bloodlessly, a tradition still honored today by the Thugs.

The action was swift. Turan wrapped the cord around Granger's neck. The second man lifted Granger's bound legs. The third man knelt on his back.

Granger didn't fight at first. Death was preferable to a living hell of torture. He had a numb expression of resignation as the cord cut deep into his neck, constricting the windpipe, choking it off . . . .

Granger wanted to die, but his body stubbornly clung to life. The fingers of his bound hands writhed. He kicked, spasmed, convulsed. His death was hard and ugly.

Vashti couldn't watch the man's final moments. When she opened her eyes again, Turan was removing the *ruhmal* from the dead man's neck, and the Thugs vented a great collective sigh. Vashti knew she would never forget that sound.

Smiling, the priest nodded, prompting his flock to intone their mantra one more time.

"KALI MAYI KI JAI!"

The cry shook the roof beams.

Granger had been strangled on a square piece of cloth spread on the floor. His body was now wrapped up in it, then two men carried it out of the hall.

The ritual reached its peak. "We commend this soul to your charge, O Kali," the priest intoned. "To set the seal on our offering, Dark Mother, we now partake of the sacred Goor."

Again the Thugs sighed as one.

A wooden cabinet stood against the wall, below the tapestry. After making obeisance to it, the priest opened the doors and took out a black lacquered box, not unlike a safe-deposit box in size and shape.

The Thug communicants formed up in a line. The priest opened the box. It was filled with gritty, gray-black powder, the sacred Goor. He spooned out a carefully measured mouthful of Goor for each worshipper. Each communicant licked his spoon clean with much ecstatic rolling of eyes and smacking of lips. Then they all sat down on the floor in the lotus position, forming a circle. When the last of them had received a spoonful, the priest had his. Then he joined them in the circle.

Soon the Thugs began to rock and sway, as if keeping time to music only they could hear. Their heads bobbed and rolled, their eyes shut, their open mouths ecstatically moaning. They enjoyed a mass trance. Some began groaning and writhing in paroxysms of pure delight.

Vashti decided that this was as good a time as any for her to make her exit. She retraced her route to the room where Granger had originally been kept. Outside, the guards had finished their cigarette break and had moved on to some other part of the grounds.

Vashti retied her rope so it had a slipknot. She hooked her legs over the balcony rail, put her weight on the rope, and slid down on it. When her feet were safely on terra firma, she worked the slipknot. The noose came apart and the rope fell to her. She coiled it and made her escape undetected.

And that might have been the end of it, if it hadn't been for Narayan. Vashti's brother eagerly awaited the outcome of her expedition, having sobered up somewhat since she had last seen him. He refused to believe her when she told him that the prospective job had failed to pan out. He thought she was holding out on him so she could pull the job herself and keep all the loot.

Vashti told him about the Thugs. He didn't believe that, either, not at first. Ugly accusations were hurled back and forth, escalating into a screaming match.

Narayan became a believer when the spotter who originally fingered the job disappeared. In a way, that was worse. Vashti had made the mistake of telling her brother about the jewel-encrusted gold statue of Kali, inflaming his imagination with greed. Why, if he had only a few good men, what riches could be had! he thought.

He did not discuss his schemes with the rest of the clan. Narayan fancied himself a mastermind who could put it all together without the help of his doubting, naysaying brothers.

He went out to Connaught Circle, making the rounds of the watering holes frequented by his larcenous friends. His words painted glowing pictures of the riches waiting to be plucked, images so fantastic that they were not believed.

But they were overheard, and by the wrong people.

Chilled by a premonition, Vashti went looking for Narayan, a search that ended in the Café Blib. The Thugs had found Narayan first.

Vashti ran for her life. She ran all the way to the Takore family's splendid home in a fine residential district.

Again she was too late, but this time her lateness worked to her benefit. She arrived just after a police squadron had raided the place. They had swarmed through the house, the grounds, and the street, carrying away precious objects, looting the premises on the pretext of gathering evidence. They tore up the floorboards and broke down walls and dug holes in the yard in their search for treasure.

A few frantic phone calls gave Vashti the details of the catastrophe. An anonymous tipster had notified the law that they could catch the Takores red-handed. Proceeding to the address given them by the unknown voice on the telephone, they surprised the brothers while they were plundering the mansion of a wealthy businessman.

Honor among thieves? Vashti wasn't risking her life on the fidelity of her family's many friends and associates in the robber's trade. Just as the tide of fortune had turned against the Takores, those false friends would turn on her, giving her up to the law or, worse, to the Thugs.

Vashti took it on the run, with only the clothes on her back and the small change in her pockets. She didn't do too badly. She got as far as Varanasi before her luck ran out.

She was penniless and starving. She tried to pick the pocket of a Bombay merchant, but her hand had lost its cunning. He caught her and held her long enough for some nearby policemen to collar her.

She was arrested and thrown into Mulag Gaol. She hadn't been charged with any crimes. Given the lumbering pace of India's unwieldy machinery of justice, she could rot in a cell for a year before being brought up before a magistrate.

The Thugs moved faster. They had reached inside Mulag Gaol to get her.

"They wanted to take me alive," Vashti said. "They were going to bring me back to the *kalighat* and offer me up as a sacrifice. I thought all was lost, but then you came along, Nick. You saved my life, you—"

Vashti broke off her words as Carter stood up and walked toward the door. "Wait!" she demanded. "Where are you going?"

"I have to make a phone call," Carter said. "I'll be back soon."

He went out the door and hurried downstairs.

"What's up, Nick?" Pete Barnes said.

"I'm ready to talk to Hawk now."

EIGHT

The security cockpit was a technophile's heaven. The windowless room was crammed floor to ceiling with ultrasophisticated telecommunications equipment. One wall was studded with banks of TV screens, the "eyes" of the safe house's security surveillance system. But the closed-circuit video cameras providing windows into every room of the house, the grounds, and the neighborhood were only part of the picture. Other windows were equipped with infrared heat detectors, electric-eye beam grids, and sound and motion sensors.

The security cockpit lived up to its name in another way, too. It was a last redoubt, the ultimate bolt-hole in case of overwhelming attack. Its walls were foot-thick steel-reinforced concrete, as hard to break into as a bank vault's. The icing on the cake was a shielding of half-inch-thick armor plate on the inside. The room, once sealed, was airtight and supplied with its own independent oxygen system with enough air to keep a man alive for twenty-four hours.

It was not the array of protective devices that interested Nick Carter, however, but rather the massive communications console dominating the space.

The console vaguely resembled an old-fashioned Wurlitzer organ of the sort once found in the huge, ornate movie palaces of yesterday. Instead of a keyboard, the console featured a mass of switches, dials, keys, and digital readouts.

Pete Barnes sat in a chair at the console, working the combination of keys and cues that would connect the Killmaster with the AXE offices in Washington, D.C. Like all of AXE's state of the art telecom equipment, the console was rigged with a protective fail-safe device. Any attempt by unauthorized personnel to access it would cue a white-hot incendiary device, reducing those intricate, elegant components to a mass of smoking slag.

Waiting for the linkage to be established, Carter luxuriated in the cool comfort of the cockpit. "Pete, this is the best room in the house."

Barnes grinned over his shoulder. "Like it?"

"I love it. This is the most comfortable I've been since I got off the plane."

"This place has to be cool. If the mercury in the thermometer goes too high, the computers shut down." Barnes affectionately patted the console. "This baby has to be pampered. Not like us, huh?"

Relays clicked into place, banks of switches were automatically thrown, and the connection was made. The humming console vented a beep, and a green light came on.

Barnes pushed back his chair and stood up. "She's all yours," he said.

"You don't have to work any controls," Barnes explained as Carter sat down at the big board. "She's ready to go. Just carry on a normal conversation as if you were talking on the phone. The mike's pickup is very good, so don't feel you have to shout. And whatever you do, don't fool with the controls."

"I'm all set, Pete. Thanks."

"Meanwhile, I'll go see what I can rustle up in the kitchen. I'm a pretty good cook, you know!"

Carter had always liked Barnes, and he really appreciated how the man had made a graceful exit just then. This conversation was to be strictly private, and Barnes knew it.

A toneless voice emanated from the speaker: "N3, this is AXE Com-Sat, now switching you over to the director's private line."

"Thank you." Carter didn't know if he was speaking to a human operator or a computerized voice-response.

After a pause in which the speaker remained silent, Carter said, "Agent N3 to Hawk, come in please."

Hawk's voice came crackling back. The rasp was in his gruff voice, not in the telecommunications system. The head and founder of AXE sounded as near and clear as if he were in the same room.

"Have you got some answers for me, N3?"

"Here's what I've got so far, sir."

Swiftly but with the important details, Carter gave Hawk the grim facts as he knew them: the Delhi strike, which caused CIA man Deke Granger and his four-person staff to vanish overnight, had been committed by a sect of Thugs.

At the end of his report, Carter dropped his bombshell. "The Thugs carried out the action, but it was masterminded by Sergei Rogov."

"Rogov?" Hawk pondered that for a moment. "You're absolutely sure it was Rogov?"

"Yes, sir. I've got an eyewitness description that fits him to a T. You know how vain Rogov is about his appearance. He never uses disguises. This is him, no question about it."

"Son of a bitch!" Hawk exploded. A moment passed before he continued, more calmly, "Well, that explains a lot of things. We'd heard he'd been active in a few trouble spots down there, adding fuel to assorted political fires. I had a report just yesterday locating him in the northwest, in the Punjab."

"Granger must have been on to something big to bring Rogov down to Delhi," Carter suggested.

"Yes, something big," Hawk agreed. "I'm going to see if I can find out what that something is. Don't go away, Nick. I'll get back to you ASAP."

"Yes, sir," Carter said, but Hawk had already closed down the connection.

While he was waiting for the return call, Carter wandered in search of Pete Barnes. He found him in the kitchen.

"Join me for a beer, Nick?"

"Sounds great."

The two AXE agents sat down and sipped their cold brews. Barnes looked out the window at a small thermometer attached to the outer frame.

"It's a hundred and seven and still climbing."

Carter shook his head. "I don't know how you can stand this kind of heat on a steady basis." He thought briefly of his assignment in Iceland.

Barnes grinned. "It's usually not like this. This is the worst time of the year. It's always hell right before the monsoon. And this year it's even worse because the monsoon is late. Actually, today is pretty mild. It won't go more than one-twelve."

"That's mild?"

"It beats the one-twenty we had just before you arrived," Barnes said with a laugh.

The console sounded a warning buzzer, alerting them to an incoming signal. But the call wasn't from Hawk; it was from Guptil Gucharvi calling from a pay phone in downtown Delhi, the call routed through the console for confidentiality.

"How's tricks, Guptil?" Carter asked.

"As you Americans say, I have some good news and some bad news. How do you want it?"

"Bad news first."

"There was a shake-up at Mulag Gaol," Guptil said. "To everyone's surprise, the warden handed in his resignation. For health reasons, he says. And guess who just became warden?"

"Our good friend Dutta."

"Right you are. The warden's out, but so are the two henchmen we caught, the fat woman and the 'doctor.' "

"Run that by me again," Carter said.

"They were released this morning, and guess who let them go?"

Carter didn't need to have a picture drawn. "Our good friend, now Chief Warden Dutta."

"Again, right."

"It's easy enough to figure out," Carter said. "They all cut themselves a private deal. Dutta had the goods on the warden and blackmailed him into stepping down. Then he cut himself an extra slice of the pie by selling the stooges their freedom."

"That's how I see it too," Guptil agreed.

"How about the good news?"

"I got the Takores released."

"Good work!" Carter said. "How'd you do it?"

"It was easy, Nick—all it took was money. This time I did as you suggested and bought the top men in the prison system instead of the underlings. Or I should say, *you* bought them, since you're the one who's paying."

"How much did it cost me?"

Guptil told him.

Carter groaned.

"Hey, it wasn't easy finding the right wheels to grease. It seems like every official in town is taking his vacation this month."

"Oh, well, you get what you pay for."

"And wait until you see what you paid for, Nick. Those Takores are trouble! They've got one brother dead and another in the hospital. They're ready to kill somebody."

"That's just how I want them."

"Careful, Nick. They don't seem too particular about whom they kill."

"Thanks. Your warning is duly noted," Carter said. "Is the meeting set?"

"Tonight at nine o'clock. Here's the address."

Carter wrote down the location and the directions how to get there, then read them back to Guptil. Suddenly a red light flashed and a buzzer sounded. "I have to go now, Guptil. See you tonight."

"Okay, Nick."

Guptil's connection was broken and the incoming beam was cued. Hawk was back on the line.

Hawk's opening was oblique. "How's the weather, Nick?"

"It's murder, sir." Carter was wary. Hawk wasn't one for small talk.

"Plenty hot, is it?"

"Brutal."

"Then this is your lucky day. You're taking a trip to the mountains, Nick. You're going to the Punjab. Specifically, to Mhoti in Kaliapur. I understand it's nice and cool up there. And you'll find it very interesting."

"Rogov, sir?"

"Right. The something big that Rogov is up to? Well, you're going to find out what it is and derail it."

"But Rogov's down here—" Carter began.

"I want Rogov!" Hawk snapped. "You know that. But I also want his whole operation rolled up. There are some angles to this thing that you don't know yet, Nick. But Inspector Bhalk will fill you in on them."

"Inspector Bhalk? Who's he?"

"He's a top crimebuster who used to be the head man of the national Crime Investigation Bureau. Now he's on special assignment, working directly for the prime minister."

"Impressive credentials," Carter said. "But where does he fit in?"

"For the last six weeks he's been working the Punjab beat, closing in on Rogov from that end. If you two put your heads together, it won't be long before Rogov is squashed. It *can't* be long," Hawk added. "Time is running out up north. The Punjab is ready to explode."

Carter said diplomatically that he was sure Bhalk was a top man, but that he much preferred to work solo.

"This is a real opportunity for us to develop some topflight connections and good will in the very highest echelons of the Indian government, Nick," Hawk said. "Officially, India is a leader of the so-called nonaligned nations. In reality, she's been cozy with the Soviets. Until now, that is.

"Unlike his predecessors, the new prime minister doesn't believe that socialism is the best way to develop his country. He's been making overtures to our side. That's made him a wee bit unpopular with the Kremlin and with the communists in his own government. We don't want to lose him."

"The situation is that serious?" Carter asked.

"With Rogov stoking up the coals? What do you think?"

"I think I'm taking a trip to the mountains, sir."

"You got it. You'll be on your way as soon as you complete the Delhi component of your mission."

"You want me to continue here?"

"Hell, yes! We're not taking the death of those men lying down! And no pack of religious nuts—and I think it's a lot more than that—is going to kick around the CIA," Hawk said. "That privilege is reserved for Congress and the press."

Carter chuckled in spite of himself. Hawk's views on investigative committees and media watchdogs were often unprintable.

"When can you move on the Thugs, Nick?" Hawk asked.

"It'll be all over for them in thirty-six hours, sir."

NINE

The Takore family reunion took place that evening in a sixth-floor office of a commercial building in downtown Delhi. Guptil Gucharvi served as referee.

As soon as he set eyes on Vashti, Gurchuran Takore slapped her face.

He was the muscle of the clan, the second eldest brother, a black-bearded powerhouse. He didn't say a word to his sister; he just walked up to her and hauled off with an open-handed slap. The slap was so loud it made Carter's ears ring. He could imagine how Vashti's head felt.

Vashti had moved her head before the blow hit, taking some of the force out of it. But it made her stagger and almost fall. Gurchuran raised his arm for a second round. His palm whistled through the air but never reached its target.

There was a slap, all right, the sound of Nick Carter's block deflecting the strike. Gurchuran never knew what hit him. One second he was looming over Vashti, and the next second Carter had somehow come between them. Carter knocked aside Gurchuran's slap. Then he punched Gurchuran in the stomach, knocking him down.

The Takores gasped their surprise. Their brother was so strong, so brutish, that they themselves had nicknamed him "Gurchuran the Gorilla." They might have seen him knocked down sometime before, but they really couldn't remember when.

Surprise turned to anger. It was all very well for those in the family to slap one another around, but for an outsider to do it to one of their own . . . .

Gurchuran sat up, shaking his head to clear it. "You struck me," he wheezed.

"That's right," Carter said quietly. "And I'll do it again if you don't behave."

"You struck me," he repeated, dumbfounded.

Guptil sighed. It wasn't as if Carter hadn't had plenty of advance warning. Before the meeting, Vashti had a little chat with him. She explained that her brothers were not as tolerant and broad-minded as she. They would not take kindly to the discovery that their only sister had become friends with a foreigner. Plus the fact that the foreigner was possibly some kind of policeman.

Carter told her that he understood the situation, and indeed he did. Vashti Takore would have to live with her family long after he had quit the scene. And quite a family they were, too.

Sanjay Takore was the eldest brother and the head of the clan. He was thin and sharp as a knife blade. He listened more than he talked and he saw what others missed.

After Gurchuran, the next oldest brother was Dilip,

who was absent from the meeting. Dilip had been seriously wounded in the police raid, but he was recovering satisfactorily. Guptil had arranged for him to be released from a prison hospital and installed in a private clinic, a transfer that enormously upped the odds for his survival.

Next came Krishna. He was dark and fleshy, with heavy-lidded eyes, long-lobed ears, and a heavyset body. He was something of a joker, but he hadn't had much to laugh about lately.

Arum, the baby of the family, was a slim, handsome youth in his late teens, and by all accounts a rabid motorcycle enthusiast. Carter thought there might be an angle in that.

Rounding out the crowd gathered there were two genial oldsters, Uncle Topee and Aunt Asilata. Their days of active crime were long over, but they were still very much part of the clan.

And Carter needed that clan to do the job right. But he wasn't going to stand there with his hands in his pockets while Gurchuran slapped Vashti around. Gurchuran was way out of line, and Carter wouldn't put up with that kind of behavior on his team. For this was now going to be very much *his* team, and he wanted that to be absolutely understood. He was calling the shots and it was time to make that crystal clear.

So he'd knocked down Gurchuran.

Gurchuran was enraged. His cheeks flushed red with anger. The rest of his face and his bull neck turned a similar color. He bounded to his feet, and Krishna and Arum moved to back his play. Uncle Topee and Aunt Asilata stood on the sidelines, wringing their hands. Vashti sprang to Carter's side.

All the makings of a first-class donnybrook were now in place, but they never reached critical mass.

Quick as thought, Sanjay interposed himself between

his younger brother and Carter. His presence was the only thing that could have stopped the Gorilla from charging.

"Krishna! Arum! Hold Gurchuran!" Sanjay barked.

Sanjay was the boss, and when he gave the orders, they hopped to and obeyed. They grabbed Gurchuran, but they couldn't have held him back for a second if Sanjay hadn't been blocking him.

Sanjay gripped Gurchuran's shirt front with his left hand. "Are you mad?" He slapped Gurchuran with his right. "Are you utterly out of your mind?" He slapped him again.

Now that he had the Gorilla's attention, Sanjay said, "If you had an ounce of sense in that empty head of yours, you brainless brute, you'd weep for gladness that our sister is alive and safely among us!"

"If it wasn't for her, we wouldn't be in this mess!"

Sanjay slapped him again. Gurchuran could have crushed him like a flea, but he stood there and took it.

"Idiot!" Sanjay said. "Vashti's not our enemy! The Takores stand alone against those who would destroy us!"

"Not quite alone," Guptil said. It was time to acquaint the Takores with the facts of life, and they would take it better from a countryman than they would from a Westerner like Carter.

"Not quite alone," Guptil said again. "That man"—he pointed at Carter—"that man saved Vashti's life. He got her out of jail. He got you all out of jail. Listen to what he has to say. It just might keep you alive."

"But he hit me!" Gurchuran protested, sounding like an angry child. "That man hit me!"

"Okay, fine," Sanjay said. "Hit me, then, if it will make you feel better. Go on, hit me. Hit me, little brother!"

"No, no," Gurchuran said, stepping back.

"Go on! What are you waiting for? Hit me!"

"No, no. I can't hurt you, brother."

"You hurt me when you hit our sister," Sanjay said. "You hurt us all!"

"I'm sorry," Gurchuran said meekly.

"Don't tell *me* you're sorry—tell Vashti."

Gurchuran looked sheepish, like a schoolboy sent to the disciplinarian's office. His eyes were downcast and his massive shoulders slumped. "I'm sorry, sister," he mumbled. "Forgive me."

Vashti went to Gurchuran and stood on tiptoes and kissed him on the cheek. Gurchuran hugged her, breaking the tension. The others crowded forward to embrace her.

"How about that?" Carter mused. "The big lug is just a softie at heart."

"If you think that, you should have a look at his police record," Guptil said grimly. "The Gorilla is the family enforcer. He's suspected in at least a half-dozen unsolved murders."

The Takores were all hugs, kisses, and tearful smiles. Old Aunt Asilata was especially carried away with emotion. Uttering joyful cries, she rushed Vashti, throwing her arms around her, hugging her and covering her face with kisses.

Vashti had contacted her beloved aunt earlier that day, phoning her at the hideaway where she and Uncle Topee had gone underground. There was an army of fair-weather friends and underworld types searching high and low for the Takores to betray them. No Takore was safe since the Thugs had put a price on their heads.

Vashti had told Carter that she had to make sure that her aunt and uncle were safe. Carter gave the okay for her to make the call from the safe house, whose scrambled phones were untraceable. Without telling Vashti, he had Pete Barnes monitor the call.

When the call was done, Barnes shrugged, telling Carter, "I didn't pick up anything. The call was kosher."

Barnes spoke Hindustani fluently, and followed the conversation with ease. But an outlaw clan like the Takores had ways of saying more than they meant. They had developed an elaborate shorthand, a private verbal code by which seemingly ordinary, everyday references actually meant something quite different.

When Vashti declared, "You comfort me, Auntie. Seeing you tonight will ease my sorrows and extract the pain from my heart," Barnes thought it no more than an expression of endearment. He didn't know that a message had been passed right under his nose.

But Aunt Asilata knew, and acted on that knowledge.

Now, as she hugged and kissed her niece in a tender embrace, she covertly passed Vashti a small package. It was the size of a bar of soap, wrapped in rough white paper and tied with string. Vashti quickly slipped it into her pocket and no one was the wiser.

Carter said in an aside to Vashti, when the old woman had sat back down, "Don't tell me that sweet old lady is a thief, too!"

"Oh, no." Vashti smiled. "Auntie is from a different side of the family. She was never a thief."

"I'm glad to hear that."

Guptil and Barnes could have told Carter that "Asilata" is the feminine form of a phrase that translates roughly as "sword's blade." But they didn't think anything of it; a name like that in a family of criminals wasn't anything worth wondering about.

Love and harmony had been restored to the family, so now the Takores confronted Carter as a unit. Sanjay spoke for all.

"Who are you, and why do you do these things for us?" he asked Carter.

"The name's Carter, Nick Carter. I'm no philanthropist. I want something from you."

"Ah," Sanjay said, "A plainspoken man. I like that."

"Your enemies are my enemies. They killed a friend of mine. Ask your sister; she saw them do it."

"You want revenge."

"I call it justice," Carter said.

Sanjay smiled. "We Takores are not so high-minded as you. We want revenge."

"What do we need you for?" Arum said to Carter. "We can take care of them ourselves!"

"You've done a great job of it so far," Carter said. "From what I hear, you Takores need all the friends you can get. Right now, I'm the only chance you've got."

"What will you pay us?" Krishna said.

"Not a single rupee," Carter said. "I've got something that's better than money."

"What?"

"Weapons," Carter said. Then he described the kind of firepower he could supply.

That was the clincher. While the skeptical Takores wouldn't really believe it was true until they had the weapons in their eager hands, the promise of same was a powerful temptation.

"You have a plan?" Sanjay asked Carter.

"Yes," Carter said with a tight smile. "We go in shooting and we kill them all."

Gurchuran was the first to break the silence. "A good plan. I like it!"

TEN

One night later, the bearded Thug named Bharat manned his sentry post on the eagle's nest, patrolling the flat, walled-in top of the *kalighat*'s mansard roof. A widow's walk bordered the perimeter, and Bharat prowled it.

Security had been doubled and then redoubled at the temple because of the Takores, a fact bitterly resented by Bharat. Because of it, he was up here stewing in the black, humid night instead of down there in the temple. There had been a killing in the city tonight, so the sacred Goor would be made available. But not for Bharat. He was trapped on the roof, keeping this fool's vigil.

Takore? Bharat had never even heard the name until a few days before. The family didn't impress him. They lacked fight. They had found a hole in which to hide and wouldn't dare show their faces around here. But they'd wind up here all the same, tracked down one by one, stalked by the inexorable power of Thuggee. Here they would die by the *ruhmal* and be cast into the nameless river, a river whose stench polluted what there was of the night air.

There was a boat out on the river, about a hundred yards upstream from the *kalighat*. Bharat frowned. The craft looked somehow suspicious to him, and he decided it would bear watching. He didn't like the way it crept toward the landing.

Something else caught his eye, something unexpected, something long and thin and red and flickering. At first he thought it was a trick of his vision. Then he saw it again.

What was it? Heat lightning? A forerunner of the desperately awaited monsoon, perhaps?

But it was closer than the sky. It was very close. It swept across the south side of the roof. Bharat went to investigate.

About twenty-five feet away, on the other side of the lane, stood the gutted, burnt-out hulk of a ruined church. Only two walls and a tower at their juncture remained standing. The tower was a few feet taller than the *kalighat*.

A thin red line of light shone from the top of the tower, glowing like a razor-thin cut in the black body of the night.

Bharat stared at it in wonder. It stared back at him. The beam touched him. Startled, he looked down at his chest. On it glowed a red dot no bigger than a coin. It was fiery red, as red as the ruby eyes of the idol in the temple. The fire eyes of Kali.

An unseen bow twanged. Its arrow leaped the red beam. It drilled Bharat right where the ruby eye glowed. A heartbeat later the red light winked out—and so did Bharat's life.

• • •

Nick Carter unscrewed the laser guide scope from its bracket mountings on the Power-Slam crossbow. The principle was simple. The laser light mounted on the bow was the shaft's guide path. He pointed the barbed arrows at the target and loosed it where the red dot glowed.

The shot had been tricky, however, since Carter was wedged in an uncomfortable position using the church tower's roof as a firing platform.

But the shot had scored. Carter put the scope back into its padded protective case that hung on a strap around his neck. The instrument could stand some rugged treatment, but there was no point in abusing it. He'd want to use it when he reached the other side.

The Killmaster was ready to go. He wore a padded Kevlar vest, black pants, and dark sneakers. Wilhelmina was snug under his arm, her shoulder rig strapped over the bulletproof vest. Hugo was tight on his wrist, and a half-dozen tiny gas bombs were safely salted away in a well-secured pack.

He fastened the crossbow across his back, then climbed down from the roof. He wriggled through a hole and dropped down into the tower room.

He wasn't alone. Vashti and Gurchuran were with him: Vashti because she was a cat burglar skilled at working high above the ground and because she had climbed this tower before, using it as a vantage post when she had previously investigated the *kalighat*; Gurchuran because he was a killer.

They were outfitted similarly, but their weaponry was different. Gurchuran was delighted with his piece, and he had a right to be. It was a Kalashnikov automatic rifle that Guptil had somehow obtained.

Guptil was the armorer for this action. He had gone through a half-dozen illegal weapons shops, skimming

the cream to supply the Takores. Carter smiled mirth-
lessly at the sight of the AK-47, just as he did at the
Tokarev TT-33 pistol clipped to Vashti's belt. The Soviet-made weapons were going to be turned on Rogov's
hired hands. That should put the KGB in solid with the
Delhi Thugs.

"I saw your man drop. Good shot!" Gurchuran
rumbled admiringly, squeezing Carter's shoulder.

Shadows hid the Killmaster's wry grin. He understood that Gurchuran was one of those types who, if
you knock them down, will either try to kill you or be
your best friend.

Now it was Vashti's turn. Gurchuran encircled her
waist with his huge hands and lifted her up, boosting her
to the hole in the roof. Vashti wriggled up and through
it.

Topping the tower was an ornamental stone knob
about the size and shape of a soccer ball. Vashti sat with
her legs wrapped around it while she uncoiled her line. It
was a long strong rope with a grappling hook at one
end; the hook was wrapped with rubber strips to muffle
its sound. She fixed a noose in the free end, slipped it
over the stone ball, and pulled it tight.

Vashti knew that she could never make a clear cast
while sitting. She placed her feet on the narrow ornamental strip bordering the ball, then she uncoiled her
legs, rising to a crouch. Generally she was immune to
heights, but this was more than a little unsettling. She
remembered being manhandled in the prison infirmary
by Primala and her accomplice, she pictured Narayan in
the booth at the café, she thought of Dilip lying in his
bed of pain. Then the spell of queasiness passed and she
knew she could go on.

Guards now patrolled the *kalighat* with leashed dogs.
Two groups of three dogs each patrolled around the
mansion in opposite directions. Vashti made her first

cast when the hounds and handlers were hidden on the
north side of the house.

Her first cast struck the cornice of the *kalighat*, but
didn't catch and slid free. Vashti frantically hauled it
back and tried again. Another miss.

Her third try had a bit too much power to it. She
wavered, nearly losing her balance, righting after a
breathless instant. When she glanced down, the world
seemed to plummet away from her. She stopped looking
down.

But the throw was good. The grappling hook had
latched onto something, and she tested it with her
weight. If the hold was no good, it was better to find out
now rather than halfway across. She pulled and it held.
Satisfied, Vashti scrambled back up on the roof. Her
handiwork looked good to her; a lifeline linked the
church tower to the *kalighat*. She wriggled back down
through the hole and dropped lightly to the tower floor.
The rope could be reached easily from the tower's
arched window, and Vashti wanted to go first.

"I rigged the rope, so I'm the one who should test it,"
she insisted.

"I don't like to throw my weight around," Carter
said, "but since I'm the one who's paying for this party,
I'll go first."

"I hate high places," Gurchuran said. "What am I
doing up here?"

"You wanted to show us all how brave you are, my
brother," Vashti teased.

"And so I shall! So I shall!"

Carter gave himself one last going-over to make sure
all his pockets were buttoned fast, all his gear secured.
He reminded the others to do the same. He crouched on
the wide windowsill, taking hold of the rope with one
hand. The tower and the mansion were too evenly
matched in height to slide across via a pully rig. He'd

have to climb across like a monkey on a vine.

He took a last look. The boat on the river was twenty or thirty yards from the landing. Silent, lightless, it drifted along the river of sludge. The guards and dogs were safely absent. Time to go.

Carter gripped the rope in both hands, wrapped his legs around it, and pushed off from the sill. He went hand over hand, hanging with his back parallel to the ground far below. Gloves would have been easier on his hands, but he preferred direct contact with his bare flesh.

A few days earlier, he had hung over a rocky Icelandic chasm, buffeted and blasted by Arctic winds. Now he dangled spiderlike from a rope in Delhi on a night of frightful heat.

But progress had been made. This time nobody was trying to cut his line the way the KGB agent in Iceland had done. It occurred to Carter that if Gurchuran held a grudge against him, now was the perfect time to settle the score. A stroke of a knife across the lifeline would send Carter plunging straight down to his death.

This was not the first time this unpleasant thought had come to Carter, but he had factored it into his calculations. Gurchuran could kill Carter only at the price of souring the *kalighat* raid, and the Gorilla was hungry for the big Thug kill. That was the Killmaster's ace in the hole.

Still, the thought added a jolt of extra urgency to his efforts, if any was needed, and Carter finally reached the other side.

He eyed the grappling hook where it snagged the ornate balustrade. A solid hold.

The bearded sentry was dead. No doubt about that. The roof was clear. Carter fastened the laser guide scope back on the crossbow, but he didn't activate it yet.

Gurchuran came across, moving like some giant tree

sloth. He huffed and puffed and energetically worked his way across, his gear rattling and jouncing and clanking. The noise couldn't have been as loud as it seemed to Carter, since no guards looked up to investigate the racket, but the Killmaster gritted his teeth until his jaws hurt, relaxing only when Gurchuran had made his way to the relative safety of the mansion roof.

Even then he scrambled for a foothold, his shoes scuffling noisily on the cornice. Carter leaned out and lent a helping hand. The Gorilla vented a vast sigh of relief when he finally swung his legs over the rail and stood on the roof.

Vashti crossed over with the least difficulty. She was nimble and in her element now. There was no keeping her safe at home while the rest of the clan went forth to do battle. Her argument for inclusion was irrefutable: the Thugs had tried to kill her, not once but twice.

She could climb, and she could shoot, too. Carter had checked out all the Takores to make sure they could use their weapons. A basement target range provided by one of Guptil's arms dealers served as the proving ground. All the members of the family passed with flying colors. Now it was time to use those fancy weapons.

Carter could see a long way off from the rooftop. The *kalighat* grounds, the square, the nearby streets—all were laid out like a tabletop model.

The boat had drifted downriver to within a few yards of the landing. Some few streets south of the square, a lone motorcyclist followed a seemingly aimless path that gradually brought him closer to the *kalighat*. The broad avenue leading into the square carried little traffic. A panel truck was parked at the corner where the avenue intersected the square.

Headlights glowed on the avenue, slowly proceeding toward the square. The approaching vehicle was revealed to be a cherry-red, double-decker bus, its interior dark and without passengers. Those few local inhabitants out on the street must have been surprised by the bus as no bus lines serviced this decayed district.

The bus pulled over to the curb, halting not far from where the panel truck was parked. Its lights went off, blinked twice, then once more went dark.

Carter checked his watch.

"Five minutes to zero hour," he said. "Let's move!"

ELEVEN

In 1867, Earl Ponsonby, appointed special investigator by the Viceroy of India and charged with the suppression of a virulent outbreak of strangling deaths, concluded his labors by optimistically declaring, "I am confident that the abominable creed of Thuggee will be extinct within a generation."

He was wrong. The British raj had come and gone in India, but Thuggee still remained. Its practitioners were merely more circumspect than of old.

Thuggee would endure as long as India endured. So believed Gopalaswami Pandit Mukerjee, high priest of the Delhi Thugs. But changing times demand new ways. The treasure heaped high in the counting room testified to the success of those new ways.

A religious man, Pandit Mukerjee believed that piety and profit went hand in hand. It was ever the practice of the Thugs to plunder their victims. After all, it was as easy to strangle a rich man as a poor man, and far more lucrative.

When Archdale Lundy had first put forth his proposal, Pandit Mukerjee listened with interest. Lundy, a lover of the esoteric and the bizarre, had extensive contacts in the shadow world of secret cults and outlaw sects. He came to Mukerjee with an idea elegant in its logical simplicity.

Kali must be fed her diet of holy victims. The Thugs required a fresh supply of them. Since they were going to kill anyway, why not get paid for it?

Instead of selecting victims at random, the Thugs could turn a pretty penny by doing away with specially selected persons. Persons whom certain interested parties would happily pay to see safely dead.

Lundy was a contractor of murder and he proposed to enter into an arrangement with the Thugs. He would finger the victims, supplying the stranglers with all the information they needed to know to carry out their actions. The Thugs would be paid a tidy sum for each killing, and of course could keep any loot they managed to pluck from their victims. Kali would have her sacrifices.

Other, less farseeing individuals would have turned down Lundy's offer. He was not a Thug—not even a Hindu. He was, in fact, English, but he had spent most of his life in India. Forty years had passed since the British abandoned the subcontinent, but many Indians still retained bad feelings toward them.

Pandit Mukerjee was willing to take a chance. His gamble had paid off with stunning success. A succession of contract kills brought newfound prosperity to the *kalighat*. An added bonus was Lundy's intimate connections with high-level government officials and business tycoons, who themselves profited in this marketplace of murder. Their paid-for clout kept the law far from the doors of the temple.

When he got to know Lundy better, Mukerjee realized with a shock of recognition that the Englishman, too, was in his own way a disciple of death.

The killings had run the gamut, from unwanted spouses to business rivals to political candidates. Interestingly, most of the political victims were moderates and centrists, never leftists. The Thugs didn't care. They were apolitical. Their political allegiance was to the golden cord of the *ruhmal*.

The arrangement had been in place for well over a year when Lundy came to Mukerjee with a rush job. Slated for extermination was not one but five victims, a feast of offerings for Kali.

The deed—deeds—were done. It had been almost ridiculously easy to abduct the victims. They had been brought to the *kalighat* to go one by one under the *ruhmal*. The dismembered corpses were weighted down and cast into the river.

The man Granger was saved for last. Lundy's client, the Russian Rogov, interrogated him. Granger was not so forthcoming, so extreme measures were applied to make him talk. He talked. When he had said all that Rogov wanted to hear, Granger went the way of his colleagues, under the *ruhmal* and into the river. A most profitable transaction for all concerned. Except for the victims, of course.

Pandit Mukerjee had no difficulty reconciling murder with morality. Like his brethren, he considered himself a philanthropist, the Thugs a boon to all mankind.

His logic was simple. What was the ultimate threat to India? Too many people. The swarming masses in their hundreds of millions threatened to swamp authority, law, and order. Removing as many of those persons as possible was a public service.

And if such removals turned a profit, so much the better.

There had been a killing tonight, and the temple was

well filled for the occasion. The victim was an ordinary individual unconnected to Lundy. Not even Lundy's numerous contracts could supply all the needed victims.

Most of the members of the temple had come out for the ritual. They watched the murder and ingested the sacred Goor.

Goor was the keystone of the cult. The gray powder was compounded of pulverized roots, herbs, and mushrooms selected for their hypnotic and hallucinatory powers. The drug's origin was lost in the obscurity of antiquity, but Mukerjee suspected that it was the same substance as *soma*, the mind-blowing "food of the gods" so glowingly described in the ancient Aryan writings of the Rig-Veda.

Nearly forty killers now writhed ecstatically in a circle on the temple floor, Goor-transported into bliss. Flickering red and yellow lights sent elongated shadows scurrying across the temple walls.

Mukerjee's assistant had led the ceremony and distributed the Goor. Mukerjee abstained. He had business to transact, and there was no doing business with a headful of Goor.

Success created its own delightful problems. The Thugs had too much money stashed away in the *kalighat*. Mukerjee thought it was time to invest. The treasure chamber would be the scene of his calculations. He had over a dozen financial prospectuses awaiting his scrutiny.

Mukerjee was fifty, burly and dynamic. With his gleaming, hairless head and belligerently outthrust jaw, he resembled a vest-pocket Mussolini. He resembled the dictator not only physically, but in the scope of his ultimate ambitions as well.

Now he climbed the stairs to the second-floor gallery, crossing it to arrive at the sealed treasure room. He had the only key, which hung on a chain around his neck.

He unlocked the heavy door, opening it. He raised his foot to step across the threshold.

Clamorous commotion erupted in the *kalighat*'s upper floors. Shouts, shots, and screams.

A hatchway in the roof provided entry into the *kalighat*, and a ladder led down to the floor below. Carter, Vashti, and Gurchuran descended into a sprawling loft. The space was crowded with low-hanging rafter beams and transverse braces that supported a colony of roosting birds, hundreds of them. The invasion of their home provoked an explosion of raucous cries, squawkings, and fluttering feathers.

The floor was carpeted with their fetid droppings. The combination of trapped heat and stink was almost overwhelming to the humans but not to the crowd of fat, bold rats who also lived there. Some looked as big as cats. They stood on their hind legs, rubbing their front paws, ruby eyes burning, whiplike tails dragging across the floorboards. They chittered their displeasure at the two-legged intruders.

An oblong hole, coffin-shaped, gaped in the floor. It was a stairwell, and a sentry climbed the stairs to see what all the racket was about.

He stuck his head out of the top of the stairwell: "Get back up on the roof, Bharat! You're not due to be relieved for another hour yet. Hey! You're not Bharat!"

A ruby-red dot of light winked into being, shining in the middle of his alarmed face. It was followed in the same breath—the sentry's last—by a crossbow bolt that hit him right between the eyes. He fell backward and tumbled noisily down the stairs.

Carter fitted another bolt to his crossbow. He hooked the tiny twin prongs of the goat's-foot over the cable bowstring, put some muscle into it, and wrenched it back, cocking the device.

He and the Takores ran down the stairs. The dead man lay with his upper body in the stairwell and his legs stretching into the hall, which was dim, yellow-walled, and musty. Two Thugs rounded the corner and stepped into view. Sundram and Turan had come to investigate the noise.

The crossbow sang. Sundram went down, skewered neatly through the heart.

Turan opened his mouth to shout an alarm. Carter dropped the crossbow, gave his right wrist a flick, and Hugo sprang into his palm. He expertly threw the blade. A spinning silver blur wheeled across the hall, Hugo finally lodging itself in Turan's throat.

Turan tried to see what it was that had pierced his neck. When he tilted his head down to take a look, he caused Hugo's hilt to press against his chest, driving the blade deeper.

He tried to cry out—not in fear but in warning—but he couldn't mouth a word, he was choking on his own blood. He coughed, staggered, and died.

Carter pulled the blade free and wiped it clean before returning Hugo to its sheath. Finally, he stooped to pick up the crossbow. The action was getting a little too intense for it, so Carter slung the weapon over his shoulder. Wilhelmina jumped into his hand.

Around the corner was a landing and a flight of stairs. At the bottom of the stairs was another landing and a door opening onto the second floor. Carter, Vashti, and Gurchuran went down the stairs just as a trio of Thugs stepped through the door.

Gurchuran was just itching to cut loose with that awesome AK-47, and this was his moment. A deafening burst of automatic fire racketed in the stairwell as the Gorilla sprayed slugs into the newcomers. Two dropped. The third hadn't come all the way through the door, and he jumped back behind the doorframe.

The survivor screamed for help, but the shooting

sounded the alarm far more effectively than he did. Reinforcements toting guns poured into the gallery.

Gurchuran, impatient to get on with the slaughter, hurdled the rail and dropped down to the landing. His massive thighs flexed with the shock of landing. He poked the rifle muzzle out the door and sprayed the lone survivor.

Shots blasted the doorframe over his head, spraying the Gorilla's shaggy head with wood splinters and plaster. He turned to see a trio of Thugs barreling down the hall, shooting as they came. Gurchuran hosed them with the AK-47. They ran into a wall of lead and stopped dead in their tracks. Quite dead.

More shots came from the opposite direction. Grinning maniacally, Gurchuran turned his gun on them.

Nothing happened. He was out of ammo.

Vashti grabbed him by the collar at the back of his neck and yanked him back into the shelter of the stairwell before he could join the dead.

The eaters of Goor had left their trances far behind. The most clear-headed of them had already grabbed their guns and were racing up the stairs to the gallery, firing as they came, laying down a protective barrage.

The *kalighat* buzzed like a stirred-up hornet's nest. The party was rolling, but not all the guests had arrived yet.

The temple was a long rectangle whose short sides formed the entrance at one end and the altar at the other. The stairwell held by Carter and company was at the altar side. At both sides of the opposite entrance were grand staircases rising to the second-floor gallery. Riflemen now lay prone near the top of the gallery stairs, only their heads and weapons showing above the uppermost step. They laid down a lot of firepower to little effect, since few of their shots went into the stairwell.

More immediate danger was provided by a second

group stationed in the ground-floor landing of the stairwell. They fired up the shaft, their bullets shredding metal rails and punching lines of holes in the stone steps.

Carter and the two Takores were pinned down. The riflemen at the gallery stairs barred the hall. The shooters below transformed the shaft into bullet alley. None of the Thugs had a clear shot yet, but ricochets from the fusillade were even more dangerous than their carefully aimed shots.

A slug bounced off the walls, flattening itself into a lead disk against the wall a few inches to the right of Carter's ear.

The blasting increased as the shooters below laid down covering fire. The purpose of the salvo was to clear the way for some of their number to climb the stairs.

Carter, Vashti, and Gurchuran flattened themselves against the walls as bullets streamed up the shaft. The racket was thunderous, so loud that it drowned the footsteps of the skulkers making their way up the stairs. But Carter didn't have to hear them: he felt the vibrations of their feet pounding on the steps.

Gurchuran dumped his empty clip and shoved in a fresh one, an elongated banana clip holding plenty of rounds.

A foolhardy Thug tried to rush the door. He came in shooting, but he didn't hit anybody. Vashti shot him in the forehead.

The stair raiders were near. The Killmaster motioned to Gurchuran, who sidled into position, kneeling, covering the stairs.

The reckless band charged. Two could play the ricochet game, Carter thought. Gurchuran didn't have a clear shot at them, but he fired at the blank wall facing the stairs stormed by the raiders, holding down the trigger, emptying the clip. A few dozen rounds bounced off the wall, tearing up the climbers.

Carter pulled two grenades from his gear, armed them, and dropped them down the shaft. The lethal eggs exploded with a tremendous blast that wrought havoc on those below. Screams and smoke billowed up the shaft. The shooters down there wouldn't be shooting anymore.

Dull, booming concussions were heard, muffled by the walls. But they weren't echoes of the grenades thrown by the Killmaster. They came from outside. The other uninvited guests had arrived. The party swung into high gear.

Arum Takore had the most refreshing ride in town as he piloted a 500cc Kawasaki motorcycle into the square at a speed of fifty miles per hour. The wind in his face was relatively cool, and he really hated having to slow down.

The double-decker bus parked at the intersection of the avenue flipped its headlights on, illuminating the lone rider. Arum's and the bike's weirdly elongated shadows were projected on the wall bounding the *kalighat*'s western perimeter, where the main gate was.

The iron-hinged double wooden doors were closed tight. As Arum geared down, slowing, he heard gunfire coming from inside the *kalighat*. He braked to a halt in front of the stout double doors. Somebody must have been watching him through the gate, because a voice started shouting at him as he skidded to a halt.

Arum reached into his saddlebag and pulled out a satchel charge. He thumbed down the red button and heard it click into place, arming the detonator. The timer was preset for a ten-second delay. Holding the charge by its strap, Arum skidded it across the pavement. It came to a halt against the gate doors.

Arum zoomed off, speed-shifting with the throttle wide open. The bike kicked in, doing a wheelie for fifty feet before its front wheel touched the road.

A guard on the other side of the gate shoved a rifle barrel through the slitted gunport and took a bead on Arum's fast-disappearing back.

The charge exploded.

Arum was already safely out of the square, hitting nearly a hundred miles per hour by the time he rounded the corner.

The explosion smashed the gates loose from their massive iron hinges, hurling them like flipped playing cards. Their headlong flight swept several guards out of existence.

The double-decker bus rolled forward, gathering speed as it chugged across the square. High-beam headlights picked out the clouds of smoke and debris wafting upward from the hole in the wall where the gate had been.

Krishna Takore drove the stolen bus. Makeshift armor plating was rigged around the driver's compartment, with a narrow slit serving as a peephole. Visibility was poor through it, but not so poor that Krishna couldn't see the opening. The bus plowed through it, entering the grounds.

The one gate guard who survived the blast stood in front of the bus, shooting at it. The windshield imploded, showering Krishna with shards, cutting him superficially in half a hundred places.

Snarling, Krishna jerked the wheel to one side, chasing the now-fleeing guard. The guard wasn't fast enough and went under the wheels, screaming.

The *kalighat* defenders suddenly realized they were under attack from a second front. A dozen gunmen dashed out the main entrance, lined up on the portico stairs, and opened fire on the bus.

Sanjay Takore went into action. Apart from the driver, he was the bus's only passenger. He rode in the upper level, wrapped in a homemade steel-plated bunker. His traveling companion was a .50-caliber machine gun. Sanjay was a former infantryman in the Indian army, and working the stuttergun was like coming home.

He swung the weapon around on its tripod, depressed the firing studs, and raked the front of the temple with a blistering barrage of heavy-duty slugs.

The typhoon of hot lead hammered fist-sized chunks of stone out of the pillars and stairs. What it did to flesh and blood and bone was even worse.

The Thugs on the front stairs looked as if they'd been tossed into a meat grinder.

A stampede was now on by the surviving Thugs to escape with their lives. Survival-minded stranglers ran like crazy, putting as much distance between themselves and the *kalighat* as possible.

Inside, the shooters pinning Carter and the Takores in the stairwell had dwindled to a precious few. Carter decided to cut their numbers even further.

Arming a grenade, the Killmaster rolled it down the gallery like a bowling ball. The riflemen remaining on the gallery staircase saw it coming. They threw down their guns and tried to outrun it. The blast picked them up and flung them aside like tenpins.

Gurchuran sprayed the hall in the opposite direction, catching two luckless individuals who chose that moment to dash across the corridor. They ran into eternity instead.

Then Carter was in the hall with a grenade in one hand and Wilhelmina in the other. A bunch of diehards on the ground floor didn't have the sense to run for their lives. They popped some shots at him instead.

Carter ducked down behind the stone balustrade for

cover. While he was estimating the location of the diehards from the angle at which their shots hit the opposite wall, a heavy door opened to the right of him.

A skinny, mean-faced Thug stuck his head out the door. Vashti took aim and hit him. He fell forward, blocking the door with his body so it couldn't be closed.

Carter armed a grenade and tossed it overhand, flipping it over the balustrade and down in the direction where he guessed the shooters were.

The blast didn't get them—the throw went wide—but it served to divert their attention long enough for the Gorilla to get into position. He propped the AK-47 on the railing and fired down into the temple. Gurchuran had gone kill-happy. His face was a crazed mask as his gun chopped down anyone who moved in the *kalighat*.

The diehards died.

Suddenly, no one was shooting at the Killmaster and his team anymore. From outside came the occasional short burst of machine gun fire. Sanjay was mopping up.

Vashti crouched beside Carter, pointing at the room with the open door. ''There's somebody inside!''

Carter's hand closed on a grenade, but he never got to use it. The door was pushed open and Pandit Mukerjee ran out, hands held high, shouting, ''Don't shoot! I surrender!''

Carter had almost shot him, a reflex action. He held his fire when Vashti gasped, ''That's their leader!''

But Gurchuran lacked Carter's self-control. He whipped the gun muzzle around, trained it on Mukerjee, and pulled the trigger.

Nothing happened. He was out of ammo again.

But the Gorilla was not to be so easily cheated out of one more kill. Tossing his weapon aside, he sprang toward Mukerjee. Growling, he grabbed the high priest's shirt front with one hand and his belt with the other. With one clean jerk, he lifted Mukerjee off his feet and into the air. Carter moved to intercept him, but there was no stopping the Gorilla now. Lifting the screaming high priest above his head, Gurchuran hurled him off the gallery.

Mukerjee hit the floor below like a sack of stones. He died instantly, much to Carter's regret.

Carter was annoyed, but he couldn't blame Gurchuran. He would have liked to have asked the high priest of the Delhi Thugs a few questions—such as where he could find Sergei Rogov.

TWELVE

Rogov slowed the car and frowned. "What's that?"

"I'd say it looks rather like a fire, wouldn't you?" Lundy said.

"Yes, but what's it doing in the middle of the road?"

"Well, you know India, old sport," Lundy said. "These things happen."

Rogov and Lundy were proceeding east to the *kalighat* square along the main thoroughfare. They were on their way to the temple to confer with Pandit Mukerjee about the Takore problem. Rogov drove. He was proud of his driving skill and always insisted on taking the wheel when he was in a car.

The fire blazed where the avenue entered the square, effectively blocking it to all vehicular traffic. The dark, blocky shape outlined at the heart of the conflagration was the panel truck that had been parked on the corner prior to the raid.

Uncle Topee had done his work well. The stolen truck had been rigged with a thermite bomb by Carter. Uncle Topee drove it to the square, parked, and waited. When Arum bombed the gates and the bus began its attack, Topee started the truck and drove it into the middle of the street, blocking both lanes. He disconnected the hot-wired ignition, stopping the truck dead. He activated the timed detonator, preset to a sixty-second delay. The red light came on, indicating that the incendiary device was alive and ticking. Topee put his old bones into high gear as he climbed down from the cab and hurried away from the truck. One minute elapsed and the bomb blew.

Uncle Topee did not slow his pace, nor did he look back at the thermite inferno engulfing the truck. Methodically he trudged to the nearest side street, where his car was parked. Not that it was exactly his car. It had been stolen too. That was the Takore way.

He started the car and drove away, threading through a twisty maze of back streets and alleys. The only decent road into the square was now blocked by the blazing truck. It would prove quite a roadblock for any police interlopers.

Eventually, Uncle Topee's car emerged from the complex labyrinth of alleys onto a main road far removed from the scene of the action. He pointed the nose of the car toward the hideaway and drove there without further incident, exiting the scene and any future action.

Rogov and Lundy were lucky. Had they arrived a few minutes earlier, they would have been inside the temple when the Killmaster's crowd lowered the boom. But they didn't think of themselves as lucky when they saw the burning truck and heard the shouts and explosions from the *kalighat*. Rogov killed the lights, pulled over to the curb, and shut down the engine. He and Lundy got out.

The truck had just about burned itself out, but the heat was still intense. The truck was a gutted, charred shell of smoldering black metal. Patches of flaming gasoline sizzled on the blacktop, and the intersection was littered with shards of metal and glass.

The two men gave the blaze a wide berth. They found a sheltered vantage point across the street from where the main gate had been. They could see that the *kalighat* was a battlefield. Bodies sprawled on the grounds. Clouds of smoke floated past. Fire crackled, but the shooting had stopped.

Rogov drew his pistol and started forward.

"Where the devil do you think you're going?" Lundy asked.

Ignoring him, Rogov walked north, then crossed the street. Cursing under his breath, trying to look in all directions at the same time, Lundy darted after him, his body involuntarily tensed against a bullet.

Rogov hid in the shadows at the northwest corner of the perimeter wall. He started edging his way south toward the gate.

"Careful!" Lundy hissed. "We don't know what's afoot here!"

"How do you propose we find out, unless we take a look for ourselves?" Rogov snapped.

"I'd just as soon read the police report tomorrow. Speaking of which, the law is liable to come along any moment now, so I suggest we absent ourselves—"

Rogov wasn't listening. He moved forward. He walked to the gate, hidden by the wall and trailed by the reluctant Lundy. He slowly stuck his head around the corner of the massive gatepost and peered into the grounds.

A band of armed men weighed down with bags of loot ran out the main entrance of the temple. They went down the stairs and hurried along the path leading to the river landing.

Rogov made his move. Hunched low, crouched almost double, he scrambled through the portal and into the grounds, taking advantage of the drifting smoke and rubble to conceal himself.

When the cloud dissipated, Rogov and Lundy were safely inside the grounds. The numerous mounds of debris provided plenty of cover. Rogov scrambled like a broken-field runner, zigging and zagging, working his way toward the rear. The younger Lundy was hard-pressed to keep up.

The pair drew abreast of the temple just as three more raiders ran out of the building. Rogov and Lundy ducked down, hiding behind some broken masonry.

There was a woman, a big brute, and a third man. The woman and the brute were laden down with loot. Gold and jewelry sparkled in the burlap sacks slung over their backs. The third man carried a machine gun whose muzzle was in constant sweeping motion, covering the area, seeking targets but finding none.

The *kalighat* blanketed the trio in shadow as they scrambled down the path. They broke free of it for an instant when they reached the top of the stairs leading down to the river.

The woman and the big man, both Indians, meant nothing to Rogov. But it was the third man, a Western-er, whose face stunned him with the shock of recognition.

Nick Carter.

For one of the few times in his life, Rogov was at a loss. When he finally remembered the pistol in his hand, it was too late. The Killmaster had followed his allies down the stairs and out of the line of fire.

Rogov jumped up. Lundy grabbed him, trying to pull him back under cover. "Are you mad?" Lundy rasped. "They'll shoot us to pieces!"

Suddenly a cool pistol muzzle was pressed against Lundy's sweaty forehead. "Take your hands off me," Rogov growled.

Lundy obeyed.

"Never lay your hands on me again," Rogov said. "If you do, I will kill you."

Rogov walked briskly to the path. Stretched across it was a dead Thug clutching a rifle. Rogov paused to pocket his pistol and pick up the rifle, which was loaded with a nearly full clip.

Rogov hurried to the top of the long flight of stairs that ran down to the steep riverbank. At their base, the stone tongue of the landing thrust out into the black river. A power launch was moored there, its idling engines purring. Most of the raiders were already on board. Carter was helping to cast off the mooring line.

Perfect. Rogov was a marksman of note, but this was no place for sharpshooting. He flipped the weapon's selector to Autofire. He would spray the entire clip at the American.

How could he miss?

Christmas had come early for the Takores. The holiday meant nothing to the Hindu robber clan, of course. But when they finished delivering the coup de grace to the wounded Thug and discovered the treasure room, they whooped it up like a bunch of kids reveling in their gifts under the tree on Christmas morning.

The vaulted room on the second floor was filled to the brim with a variety of plunder. Fabulously intricate rugs were stacked in rolls. There were heavy pieces of antique furniture, an immense bronze astrolabe, gold figurines of household gods, and an onyx and marble chessboard whose pieces were beautifully wrought ivory representations of the gods of the Hindu pantheon.

Greed could kill the Takores where the Thugs had failed. Sanjay knew this. "Take only money, gold, and jewelry!" he ordered.

There was plenty of all three, too much for the

brothers to carry away even if they made a half-dozen
trips. Professional thieves that they were, they had come
prepared for looting. They brought out sacks with
straps and started stuffing them full of gold, jewels, and
currency.

Nick Carter manned the front entrance, sitting behind
the machine gun which had been taken down from the
upper level of the double-decker bus.

He had decided that when the police came, he was
leaving, whether the Takores were ready or not. Their
lust for loot wasn't going to lead him into a shoot-out
with Delhi's finest, and he had told Sanjay exactly that.

He thought Vashti was upstairs with the others, grabbing all she could carry, but in fact she was busying
herself at the wooden cabinet behind the statue of Kali.
A grenade had amputated one of Kali's legs and two of
her arms, as well as puncturing much of the idol's
golden skin with tiny bits of shrapnel.

Vashti opened the cabinet and found the box of
Goor. She opened the lid. The sacred dust resembled
gray volcanic ash, and smelled faintly sweet.

Vashti took out the small package that Aunt Asilata
had given her the previous evening. It contained a glass
vial sealed with a rubber stopper.

Vashti hadn't lied when she told Carter that Aunt
Asilata was not a thief. Asilata followed an altogether
different calling: she was a poisoner.

When her niece had spoken to her over the phone
from the AXE safe house, Asilata had had no trouble
divining her meaning. Vashti had said, "You will ease
my sorrows and extract the pain from my heart." The
powdered white crystals contained in the vial were the
extract of a powerful, deadly poison poetically named
Easer of Sorrow.

Vashti unstoppered the vial. Holding it well away
from her, scrupulously careful that not a grain touched

her skin, Vashti emptied the extract into the box of Goor. She threw the vial far away and closed the lid of the box. Then, holding the box tightly closed, she gave it a good shaking so that the poison would be evenly dispersed throughout the Goor.

Vashti knew how to hate. Some of the Thugs had escaped tonight. A quick inspection of their dead had failed to locate Primala or the man who posed as the doctor. No doubt other members of the sect had been absent from the *kalighat* on this night. Perhaps the survivors would return for their sacred drug. If they did, Vashti had left them something to remember her by, just as she would always remember her nightmare ordeal of fright and flight.

She was just putting the box back into the wooden chest when Krishna staggered into view, bent under the heavy load he was carrying.

"What's in there?" he called cheerily. "Anything worth taking?"

"No," Vashti replied, "only some worthless ceremonial objects."

"I think I'll take a look."

Vashti laughed good-naturedly at her brother. "Look at you! Why, you've already got more than you can carry! Don't be greedy. Let Kali have what is hers."

Krishna seemed inclined to press the point, but just then Carter squeezed off two quick short bursts of machine gun fire.

"That's the signal to go," Vashti said. "Let's get out of here!"

Bent almost double under their loads of loot, the Takore brothers and Vashti joined Carter on the columned portico. Police sirens wailed somewhere in the distance.

Carter wrenched the machine gun free from its tripod and cradled it in his arms, careful to keep the feed unsnarled. He covered Sanjay and Krishna as they scurried down the path to the landing. They were loaded down like a brace of pack mules, but they wouldn't give up so much as a coin to ease their burdens. The recent unpleasantness had dealt a heavy blow to the family fortunes, which would have to be replenished as quickly as possible. Tonight's haul would put them on easy street for a while.

One of Gurchuran's smaller pouches slipped free from its fastenings. It fell, spilling a mass of jewel-encrusted gold chains, necklaces, and bracelets. Vashti stuffed them back into the bag, picked it up, and slung it over her shoulders.

Carter wheeled to cover his back with the machine gun.

"What's wrong?" Vashti cried.

"Thought I saw something," Carter said. But whatever flicker his peripheral vision had picked up a second ago was gone. "Let's move."

They moved, Carter backing down the path, covering their retreat. The trio went down the long steep stairway to the water's edge, and Carter noticed a second boat drifting in the middle of the river, silent and dark.

Guptil Gucharvi captained the getaway boat moored at the landing. As Guptil was no gunman, he had been glad to man the boat while the others did the killing. Thinking about the final bill he would present to Carter for this night's work made him even happier.

But Guptil was worried, too. Pointing to the mystery boat—which was cautiously keeping its distance—he said, "Nick, look!"

"I see it," Carter said. "How long has it been there?"

"I don't know. I turned around and saw it a few minutes ago. Do you think it's the law?"

"If it is, I'd say they don't want a piece of this action.

But let's not stick around to find out."

"I'm ready to cast off when you are!" Guptil said.

The Takores had loaded their loot on board the boat, and Carter freed the mooring line.

Suddenly a blinding beam of white light leaped from the second boat. The searchlight was not focused on the landing, but at the terrace above the riverbank.

The beam pinned Rogov, exposing his armed figure. Dazzled by the brilliant spotlight, Rogov squeezed off a burst at where he guessed the landing was, but his guess was off by a country mile.

Lundy had come up behind him. When the light came on, Lundy threw himself off the path and hugged the ground.

Carter had already passed the machine gun into the boat, but a split second later Wilhelmina was in his hand. He squeezed off a few shots at Rogov, but the distance was too great for accuracy with the Luger. Still, some of the slugs whined so close to the Russian that Rogov was forced to hit the dirt beside Lundy.

Carter jumped into the boat, and Guptil opened up the throttle wide. The stern dug into the water, carving an arc as it sped away from the landing and into the middle of the river. The boat zoomed downstream.

The searchlight winked out.

"Who's that?" Sanjay shouted so he'd be heard over the motor's road.

"I don't know!" Carter said. "But it looks like they're on our side!"

The mystery boat started up, following Carter's party. It was low-slung, sleek, and fast, and had no trouble keeping up. The craft maintained a twenty-five-yard distance between itself and Carter's boat.

On the terrace, Rogov scrambled to his feet. A pair of white wakes was carved in the onyx river by the fleeing boats. Furious, Rogov emptied the automatic rifle in their direction, spraying fiery red tongues into the black body of the night. The night was the only thing he hit, however, because the boats were long gone. But Rogov stopped firing only when the clip was out of ammo.

Lundy was shaken more by Rogov's irrational behavior than by their narrow escape. Rogov was a cold-blooded artist of destruction, and Lundy had never seen him like this. The Russian was out of his head with rage.

This worried Lundy greatly. Hotheads are unreliable, and if there was one thing Lundy shunned like the plague, it was working with unreliable people.

Rogov would bear watching.

Rogov threw the empty weapon away. It clattered down the stairs.

"The game's not over yet," he muttered. "I'll see you in the Punjab, Killmaster."

Heat lightning flickered over the river. Some flashes were so bright, it almost seemed like day. Carter glanced at his watch and grinned to himself. It was almost thirty-six hours on the dot from the time he had told Hawk he would have the Delhi component of his mission wrapped up.

Guptil wove a devious route, leaving the main trunk of the river for its side channels, going down obscure branches, doubling back, threading the trackless maze of waterways that honeycombed the city. But the mystery boat stayed on their trail.

"Don't lose them," Carter said. "I want to find out who they are."

"That's good, because I can't shake them anyway," Guptil muttered.

Krishna patted the weapon cradled on his lap. "If they want trouble, I'll make some—with this!"

"They saved our necks, whoever they are," Carter reminded him. "We'd better find out who they are before we start blasting."

"Let's find out now, before they follow us to the hideout," Sanjay said.

That made sense. Guptil looked for a location for a rendezvous. He found one between two pilings under a cantilevered railroad bridge whose skeletal ribwork stood out against a sky flickering with lightning.

The slowing boat churned up white water. Guptil spun the wheel, bringing his craft around in a 180-degree turn so it faced the oncoming mystery boat prow-first, presenting the smallest target.

The Takores, and Carter, too, had their guns at the ready while waiting to discover if they faced friend or foe. After all, the other boat's action with the search-light might have been a clever ruse to disarm their suspicions.

"Don't get trigger-happy," Carter cautioned. "But don't be too trusting either."

Their pursuer backwatered to a halt. A small, high-speed craft, it held two occupants. The pilot was a woman. Standing next to her, holding the gunwale for balance, was a short, slight fellow in a white linen suit.

He put a hand beside his mouth to amplify his call: "No shooting, please!" He made his request twice, first in Hindustani, then in English.

"Identify yourself!" Carter called back.

"Ah! Mr. Carter, yes? So pleased to meet you at last. Please allow me to introduce myself," the thin man said. "I am Inspector Bhalk."

THIRTEEN

Hawk would have his little joke. It was cool in the mountains, all right, a "cool" ninety-five degrees in the midday sun.

Carter's train was stuck a few miles east of Mhoti Station in the heart of Samsirbad district in the Punjab. For two hours it hadn't moved; it just sat there on the tracks, broiling under the pitiless sky.

Earlier, at dawn, Carter and his two traveling companions had boarded a private jet at a small airfield outside Delhi. The sun was just rising, but already the heat was stifling. The sullen saffron sky showed a pale pink tint at its eastern horizon. Birds sat still in the branches of the flame trees bordering the runway. A short distance beyond the landing field lay a handful of mud huts whose inhabitants paid no attention to the sleek JetStar as it lifted off.

The jet became airborne just as the sun broke the horizon. Sunbeams silvered the sleek streamlined aircraft, making molten its needle nose, its slim drag-suppressant fuselage, its sweptback wings. The JetStar arrowed northwest, leaving behind the baking plains on either side of the Ganges. Its destination lay some 140 miles distant.

Presently, the terrain unrolling far below changed. The cracked brown plains tilted upward, steadily elevating the tableland. Long, rocky ridges thrust into view, becoming taller and more extensive the further the plane arrowed into the northwest. Soon the flatlands were replaced by rugged highlands.

A welcome touch of color gladdened the eye as the jet entered Punjabi airspace. The rivers were like sparkling silver threads interlacing the mountain ranges. There were lush, blue-green forests and sprawling fields of yellow corn and golden wheat.

Not for nothing was the Punjab called the "Land of Five Rivers." Those priceless waterways fed the vast network of irrigation canals, spillways, and reservoirs that had transformed the state into the breadbasket of India.

Carter was discreetly eyeing the inspector's assistant, Miss Majuna Chakraboti. The slim, intelligent, dark-eyed beauty had every qualification to recommend herself to him.

Air pressure altered in the cabin as the JetStar's nose tilted downward and it started its descent. Below lay a fertile triangle of land whose boundaries were circumscribed by the cities of Firozpur, Ludhiana, and Jullundur. Meandering through the territory was the shining silver ribbon of the Sutlej River.

The jet touched down at a small airfield. They hired a car and driver to take them to the station where they would catch the train to Mhoti. The driver, a blue-turbaned Sikh, was not alone. Riding shotgun for him in the passenger seat was his brother, who held a rifle across his lap, its muzzle sticking out of the open window.

"An honest man dares not venture forth unarmed these days," the driver said dourly. "It pains me deeply that things have come to this. You are well out of this unhappy land, my friends. Where are you bound?"

"We're taking the train to Mhoti," Bhalk said.

The driver and his brother exchanged meaningful glances, and the driver shook his head. "Beware! You go deeper into the heart of the madness."

"We have no choice, so please drive on."

When they reached the small station, the driver said, "God protect you from evil men, my friends."

"There's a cheerful fellow," Carter said once he was out of earshot of the driver.

"But he's right, unfortunately," Majuna said.

Carter was ready. He was armed with the unholy trinity of Wilhelmina, Hugo, and Pierre, a miniature gas bomb anchored to his upper thigh. In his bag he had the crossbow and a few other surprises. Most of all, though, he had a bullet with Rogov's name on it.

Inspector Bhalk was quite an expert on Rogov, having had time to investigate his handiwork in the Punjabi district for the last six weeks, and he brought Carter up to date on the goings-on of the Russian and his team.

One of Deke Granger's field agents in Samsirbad had uncovered some key information about Rogov's master plan. With Rogov's two-legged hounds closing in on him, the agent had fled south to Delhi, where he passed the information along to Granger.

But Rogov had acted before Granger could pass the information along through channels to his higher-ups. He arranged for the Thugs to dispose of Granger and the other four members of Granger's staff, making a clean sweep of it.

Their disappearance might have forever remained a mystery had it not been for Vashti's chance entry into the game. Bhalk followed Granger's trail from the Punjab to Delhi, switching his attentions to the *kalighat* because of the information Hawk passed along to him.

Thanks to Vashti's astonishing discovery and AXE's fine communications network, Bhalk and Majuna had been in place in a boat on the river during the raid.

It was pointless to linger in Delhi, Bhalk had told Carter. The Delhi business was only a sideshow, a diversion from the main theater of action in the Punjab. So, here they were.

They bought three tickets for a first-class compartment on the train to Mhoti, and the train arrived on time. They boarded, and it was like climbing into an oven. They pointed out to the conductor who came to punch their tickets that there was no air conditioning in their compartment. There was no air conditioning in *any* compartment, he told them. The machinery was broken. If they liked, they could write to the railway's business office for a partial refund.

"Let's look on the bright side," Majuna said. Her English had a lilting inflection that Carter found charming. "We can be happy that it's only a short ride from here to Mhoti."

Mhoti was some twenty-five miles distant. There were a few short stops along the way, so it usually took a little more than an hour to get within a few miles of Mhoti Station.

The train halted at the foot of a long, gentle slope. Two hours later, it hadn't budged an inch. The only excuse that the conductors gave for the delay was to say, as they hurried to another part of the train, "There is a delay."

Most of the passengers got out and walked around. Some of them picnicked on the grassy embankments.

Carter thought it was a toss-up as to which was more unpleasant: baking inside the carriage, or broiling under the noonday sun.

Just when Carter was ready to pick up his bags and walk the rest of the way to Mhoti Station, the train whistle blew and the conductors motioned the passengers to reboard the train. Fifteen minutes later, the train shuddered, jerked forward, and started poking up the hill. Crawling at the painful pace of a few miles an hour, the train huffed and puffed its way to the summit.

Mhoti Station sat in a valley on the other side of the mountain, standing at the southernmost boundary of the town bearing the same name. The town proper was a jumble of white and brown cubes topped by peaked roofs and interspersed with occasional spires and domes, all wrapped up in a cat's cradle of telephone and power lines.

The railroad station and its environs was the scene of mass confusion. The cool gray stone terminal building was mobbed by hundreds of citizens of all shapes and sizes, their colorful garments forming a moving rainbow of brilliant hues. They swarmed the veranda and the loading platforms. Their numbers spilled onto the tracks and the gravel beds between them. It was as if the town of Mhoti had gathered all of its inhabitants to the railroad yards.

A common impulse animated the crowd: they all kept looking west. Their attention was focused on the far horizon, where the golden curve of the earth held a range of saw-toothed brown hills. Bright decorative banners were hung from the terminal roof, and many in the crowd wore their best clothing. But their mood was that of a holiday gone sour.

Three more trains had been shunted off the main line and sidetracked in the railroad yard. The idling trains were empty, their passengers ranged all around them. Those people looked west too.

Carter's train inched downhill at a snail's pace, jerking to a bone-jarring halt some two hundred yards from the terminal.

"That last jolt had a distinct feeling of finality to it," Carter said.

"Shall we investigate?" Inspector Bhalk suggested.

"Let's."

Carter wore a tan safari jacket, its long sleeves rolled down to cover Hugo, with a light blue shirt and loose-fitting tropical weight trousers. He slung a duffel bag over one shoulder and hefted a small suitcase. He had a free hand, so he reached for Majuna's bag.

"What are you doing?" she said.

"Just trying to be helpful."

"I can carry my own bags, thank you very much," she snapped.

Inspector Bhalk politely covered his mouth with his hand, hiding his amused smile. He knew his lovely and highly capable assistant well. Ordinarily, she was unfailingly polite. Her rudeness indicated her interest in the big American.

Studiously ignoring Carter, Majuna picked up her own bag. Carter found her less easy to ignore. She was a knockout, even in a land of exotically beautiful women.

Majuna Chakraboti was a former policewoman who had distinguished herself in a number of dangerous undercover assignments. Her work had brought her in contact with Inspector Bhalk when he was with the national law enforcement agency of the Criminal Investigation Bureau, the Indian equivalent of the FBI. When Bhalk was detached from the CIB to work directly for the prime minister, he recruited Majuna to the team.

Majuna had brains, beauty, and she was an excellent

shot, too. She looked more like a pampered beauty queen than a championship marksman, but she was anything but a hothouse flower.

Majuna was very tall for an Indian woman. Thick black hair, parted in the middle, was cut to just above her shoulders and framed her striking face. She had full brows, enormous dark eyes, a sensitive mouth, and sensational cheekbones.

She wore a lightweight tan blouse and a long beige skirt whose hem brushed her ankles. The long-sleeved blouse was buttoned up to the throat. The Sikhs are a puritanical people, and they would regard the display of a woman's bare arms as a shocking breach of decorum. So she sweated in her garments to satisfy their sense of modesty. Most probably, she mused, the effort was pointless. Since she was a non-Sikh from a big city, they would probably think she was a harlot no matter how conservatively she dressed.

Her outfit, however, failed to hide the loveliness of her high breasts, her trim waist, and the length of her long legs.

Inspector Bhalk rose. Under his arm he carried a folder not unlike those used by lawyers to hold legal briefs. The battered leather portfolio might as well have been surgically attached to him: he was never seen without it.

Bhalk was of medium height but thin to the point of emaciation. His head seemed too heavy for his reedy neck to support it. His rumpled white linen suit jacket hung from his bony shoulders as if it were draped on a hanger.

The onetime Bombay police inspector had an unusual qualification for the Punjabi mission. Savatta Bhalk was neither Hindu, Moslem, nor Sikh. He was a Parsi, descended from Zoroastrian fire-worshippers who had settled in Bombay centuries ago. In theory, his neutral-

ity in the war of Hindu versus Sikh for control of the
Punjab should have rendered him as an acceptable go-
between for the different factions. In sad truth, as he
knew only too well, it rendered him equally obnoxious
to both sides. The war drums were beating and neither
side had any use for a neutral.

With his omnipresent folder tucked under one arm,
his bag held in his other hand, Inspector Bhalk said
brightly, "Shall we go?"

FOURTEEN

Ornate red letters spelled out messages of welcome on the long white banners hung from the terminal's veranda. But there was no welcome for Carter and his party.

Inspector Bhalk, fluent in the Punjabi dialect of the area, made polite inquiries as to the cause of the delay. His questions were polite, but the people on the fringes of the crowd to whom he addressed them were not. They shied away from him with looks of hostility and suspicion, and one surly peasant spat in the dust at Bhalk's feet.

Carter immediately started forward, only to be stopped by the inspector, who grabbed his arm.

"Please don't distress yourself," Bhalk said quietly. "These people have a profound distrust of strangers."

"That should make us wildly popular around here," Carter grumbled.

"There is a group of soldiers," Bhalk said. "Perhaps they will be more sociable."

A small squad of khaki-clad Indian army soldiers stood at the sidelines, killing time. They were city boys from the south, eager to talk with a friendly face or two.

"Can you please tell me what is happening here?" Bhalk asked the young corporal commanding the unit.

"Glad to, sir. Corporal Vinobha at your service," the young man said. "The train from Yatha Hunda is four hours late."

"Is that unusual?"

Corporal Vinobha nodded. "The only thing I'll say for this shithole—begging your pardon, miss—is that the trains run on time. Or they used to, until today."

"You don't seem very concerned. What if something serious happened to the train? I have heard that there is much violence in this district."

"You heard right, sir. But there's a platoon of infantrymen riding that train." Vinobha laughed harshly. "It will take more than a band of rag-headed revolutionaries to stop it!"

"I hope your confidence is not misplaced." Bhalk indicated the colorful banners and holiday attire of the now anxious crowd. "Is there some sort of celebration taking place here today?"

"A group of doctors and nurses are coming to work at the maharanee's charity clinic. They are on that delayed train. That's what all the fuss is about. But the way they're killing each other in this district, a brigade of doctors wouldn't be enough!"

"You are referring to the Maharanee Shantal Singh Sardar?" Bhalk said.

"Yes."

Bhalk flipped open his wallet, presenting credentials that identified him as a member of the very highest echelon of the Indian government.

The young corporal idly scanned the laminated ID until its import sank in. Abruptly, he snapped out of his casual posture, coming to ramrod-straight attention. Before he ordered his slow-on-the-uptake squad to follow suit, Bhalk stepped in.

"As you were, Corporal. And please, no salutes. I wish to attract as little attention as possible."

"Very good, sir!"

By now, Vinobha's unit had formed themselves into some semblance of military order. They finally got the idea that Bhalk was some kind of big shot.

"My associates and I would like to enter the terminal," Bhalk said. "However, I fear we would not make much headway in this crowd. Perhaps you and your men would be so good as to escort us."

"Yes, sir!"

"And please, Corporal, exercise politeness and consideration for others as we advance. We wouldn't want to alienate these good people with a display of bad manners."

"No problem there, sir." Vinobha flashed his cocky grin. "They already hate our guts!"

The squad formed up in a wedge, with Vinobha taking the point. Bhalk, Majuna, and Carter followed in their wake. The crowd reluctantly made way for the soldiers, who moved slowly and carefully, constantly excusing themselves for any inconvenience they might have caused. It was strange behavior for the troopers, who would just as soon have bulled their way through.

Bhalk briefed Carter on the salient facts of the conversation, which had been conducted in fast-paced Hindustani. When he was done, Carter asked, "Who is the maharanee?"

"A most unusual woman," Bhalk said. "Within living memory, her ancestors were the absolute masters of the district. Her title is now strictly honorary, of course, but she still retains much support. She's fabulously wealthy, a philanthropist of note. A Sikh herself, she has insisted that all her charitable good works be made available to Sikh and Hindu alike. Many consider her to be a major force for peace in this troubled land," the inspector concluded.

Having thanked Corporal Vinobha for his assistance and promising that it would be duly noted with his superiors, Bhalk, Carter, and Majuna made their way to the second floor of the terminal. Here was the control center of the railroad's communication network, a sprawling office now riotous with confusion and shouting.

Barring the door to the control area was an intimidating pair of guards. Their tightly wrapped turquoise turbans, flowing black beards, silver wrist bangles, knee-length breeches, and swords at their sides marked them as Sikhs.

Making up less than two percent of the population of India, the Sikhs are a proud, religious, militant people. Today they comprise a goodly portion of the Indian army, a fact that has made the government quite anxious in light of the recent disturbances that have rocked their home state of Punjab. Not for nothing does every Sikh male bear the name of Singh—"lion."

These two Sikh guards belonged to a private army. Their white tunics and breeches were trimmed with red piping, and a red sash circled the waist. Strapped over their livery were black patent leather Sam Browne belts. On their right hips hung holstered revolvers; on their left hips, they wore the *kirpan*, the traditional Sikh sword.

The duo stepped forward, standing shoulder to shoulder to bar access to the door.

"Excuse me, please," Bhalk said. "We would like to see the stationmaster."

One guard had a crescent-shaped scar spanning his forehead, left eyebrow, and cheekbone. He would have looked fierce enough without it.

"Go away!" he ordered.

Ghalk displayed his credentials, but the guards were not impressed. The other guard, the one without the scar, said, "That means nothing to me. I cannot read."

"I can," his partner said, "and it means even less to me. Now, go away, little man, and stop making a nuisance of yourself."

Bhalk didn't give up. "Perhaps you would be so good as to summon the stationmaster, so that I might speak to him."

Scarface shook his head with the air of a man whose long-suffering patience is being sorely tried. "You don't hear very well, do you, little man? I told you to go away. Go while you still can."

Casting a scornful glance at Majuna, Scarface added, "And take your whore and your kept dog with you."

The twin red spots of color blazing in Majuna's cheeks alerted Carter to the fact that what Scarface had just said wasn't very nice. That was fine. The Killmaster wasn't feeling very nice either.

The other guard didn't want to be outdone. "Go on, get!" he snarled, shoving out a heavy hand to straight-arm Bhalk in the chest.

Carter reached to pull the skeletal inspector out of range of the blow, but he needn't have bothered. Bhalk easily stepped to the side, avoiding it.

Scarface snickered, further annoying his partner, who had just lost face by being unable to tag a sickly-looking fellow who seemed to have one foot in the grave. The angry Sikh cocked his fist to throw a haymaker.

Carter moved, stepping inside the punch, tossing off a casual left-handed circular block that effortlessly deflected the fist. But the block was only part of a one-two combination. The second half of it was a spear thrust delivered with his open right hand. The blow landed under the guard's diaphragm, sinking deep.

It took the starch out of the guard's sails. Eyes bulging, face going green, he doubled forward, his mouth a wide black hole sucking for breath. He didn't have enough breath left in him for a gasp. Holding his gut with both hands, he fell to his knees in the middle of the floor.

Scarface stopped snickering. A burly, slab-shouldered bull of a man, he lunged at Carter, who sidestepped the rush, grabbed Scarface's arm, and flung him forward in the direction he was going.

There was a satisfying crunch as Scarface hit the wall headfirst. It sounded worse than it was, since the layers of his turban served as a sort of shock absorber, cushioning the skull beneath.

Scarface wasn't knocked out, but there wasn't much fight left in him, either. He sprawled on the floor, holding his head in his hands. He was blank-eyed and slack-jawed.

Carter looked back over his shoulder. The other guard had recovered enough to make trouble. His hand scrabbled at the buttoned-down flap of his holster, reaching for his gun. He was still reaching when Majuna kicked him in the belly with the pointed toe of her shoe.

The guard was back down on his knees, retching.

"Khaitan! Balindra! What are you doing?"

The words rang out in a tone of command, the voice of one accustomed to having her orders obeyed. Carter eyed the woman who stood framed in the doorway, her agate eyes flashing as she took in the scene of the two guards on the floor.

Scarface groaned, then his eyes came back into focus. Their gaze fastened on his own holstered gun.

The woman had followed his glance. "Khaitan, stop!"

She didn't shout. She barely raised her voice. But the hand that had been creeping toward the gun butt jerked back from it as if it had been burned.

The scarred Sikh named Khaitan was tough. He stood up, no mean feat considering the way his head must have felt after smashing into the wall. Carter figured the man would spend the rest of the day with one hell of a headache.

A number of individuals stuck their heads out of open doors to investigate the disturbance. It must have made quite a tableau: the stunned Sikh guards; the skeletal Inspector Bhalk; the beautiful Majuna with her nostrils quivering and her eyes flashing fire; and the Killmaster himself.

And, of course, the woman.

She cut quite a striking figure. She was small, slim, and elegant. Her mahogany-colored hair was pulled back and worn in a knotted chignon at the nape of her neck. The fine features of her face were molded with exquisite delicacy. Her honey-toned skin was flawless.

The color of her remarkable agate eyes was hard to pin down. They seemed gold, gray, green, and blue, all at the same time. Carter had never seen anything quite like them.

Her age was hard to pin down too. Her face seemed forty, except around the eyes, which were wrapped in a fine network of minute, delicate lines. Her figure seemed that of a woman of thirty, with firm breasts, a flat stomach, and slim thighs. But it was her air of authority that led Carter to guess that she was closer to fifty.

She wore a deceptively simple Western-style dress that suited her perfectly. The style was plain and unadorned; but it was a rich mauve color that might have been overpowering for most women, but not for this exotic beauty.

Layers of delicate gold chains encircled her neck.

Gold bracelets wrapped her wrists. And if the diamond on her ring finger was real—and Carter guessed it was—it was one for the record books.

But the diamond couldn't hold a candle to those piercing agate eyes that now took in the scene.

Her gaze passed over the guards, paused at Inspector Bhalk, moved on to Majuna. In one glance she sized up Majuna, estimated her place in the scheme of things, and dismissed her from consideration as a rival.

Then she took a look at Carter, a good look. She liked what she saw. She liked the intense challenge in his dark eyes, and frankly admired his tall physique.

"You are English?" she asked in English.

"American," Carter replied.

"You have come a long way to fight with my men."

"They started it."

She was amused. "And you finished it, eh?"

"Something like that."

Khaitan spoke English, too, enough of it to tell Carter, "It is not finished yet!"

"Khaitan!" the woman spoke sharply.

Khaitan bowed his head. "Ten thousand pardons. I am so ashamed."

"You know I won't stand for my men engaging in public brawling. Nor private brawling," she added. "Help Balindra attend to himself."

"But, Maharanee, who will guard you?"

"I am perfectly safe," she said. "Now, go!"

"Your wish is my command." Khaitan bowed low. Careful not to touch the other's soiled garments, he assisted his comrade to his feet. Balindra still hadn't recovered. He was bent forward, holding himself, gasping. Khaitan held him by the arm, supporting him. He escorted him to the washroom, with Balindra shuffling forward, stooped and shaky as a very old man.

"Excuse my boldness," Inspector Bhalk began, "but

you are the celebrated Maharanee Shantal Singh Sardar, yes?''

Shantal took note of Bhalk, favoring him with a regal smile. ''You have heard of me?''

''Indeed, yes. Many speak of your good works, Maharanee. And I am delighted to discover that the reports of your beauty are not exaggerated.''

The smile widened. ''You are very gallant—but I do not know your name.''

''Please allow me to introduce myself. I am Inspector Savatta Bhalk.''

''Ah, an inspector! That is quick work! Perhaps you would be so good as to tell me what has become of the train.''

''An inspector, yes, but not for the railroad, alas. I am an inspector for the Bureau of Agricultural Development, lately arrived from Delhi to conduct a survey of irrigation in your district. This is my assistant, Miss Majuna Chakraboti.''

Shantal Singh Sardar favored Majuna with a condescending smile.

''So pleased to meet you, Maharanee,'' Majuna said.

The maharanee ignored her, returning her attention to Carter. ''And who is this handsome fellow?''

''The name's Webster, ma'am, Harry Webster,'' Carter said. Determined not to be outdone in the gallantry department, he took hold of the maharanee's hand and kissed it. It was cool and dry. The Killmaster didn't have Emily Post on hand to elucidate the proper way to greet an Indian maharanee, but he had his own brand of etiquette when it came to women, especially beautiful ones. He couldn't have been too out of line, since the maharanee seemed to appreciate the gesture.

Majuna looked daggers at Carter.

''Are you an agricultural inspector, too, Mr. Webster?'' Shantal asked.

"No, ma'am. I'm a financial advisor for the Beckhoff Group. Perhaps you've heard of us?"

"Frankly, no."

"We're a consortium of independent commodities brokers, trading in futures—you know, like grain and corn shipments. This area is a leading producer in the world wheat market, so my group sent me here to survey the prospects for this season's harvest."

"Fascinating." Shantal's tone implied, subtly, that it was anything but.

Carter went on. "Mr. Bhalk here has been good enough to let me accompany him on his rounds. It's a big help for me, since I don't speak the language."

"You handle yourself very well."

"Oh, you mean that little to-do? When I was a kid I served a hitch in the army. I learned how to take care of myself there."

"Indeed," Shantal said, "Khaitan is no ordinary fighting man. He's one of my best."

"Guess I was just lucky today," Carter said with a straight face. "By the way, I'm sorry for the trouble. All we wanted to do was see the stationmaster, but there was a failure in communication."

"I'm afraid that I'm the one who must apologize, Mr. Webster," Shantal said. "Khaitan and Balindra are Djanjeri tribesmen, fierce mountain fighters who have served my family for generations. Even in this modern day, they insist on upholding their ancient tradition of protecting the Singh Sardars. Unfortunately, they are often overly zealous in carrying out their duties, especially in these uneasy times."

She beckoned them into the office. "But where are my manners, standing in the hall and talking like this? Please do come in."

The enormous room was a scene of tumult as harried railway officials fought to cope with the many problems caused by the missing train. Phones rang unanswered.

Other phones served as receptacles for torrents of abuse as near hysterical dispatchers tried to discover the whereabouts of Train 429 out of Yatha Hunda. Activity was particularly frantic at the half-dozen blackboards on which were chalked the arrival and departure times of all the trains on the line. The arrival times were being constantly pushed back.

An extraordinarily good-looking, beautifully dressed young man came rushing up to the maharanee's side. He had the profile and bearing of a Bombay matinee idol.

"This is Ashwin Naidu, my confidential secretary," Shantal said.

Majuna sniffed. Carter knew what she was thinking. A mature woman didn't keep a handsome younger man like Naidu around just to give him dictation.

As Naidu was introduced to each of the newcomers in turn, he made a little bow and said, "So happy to meet you."

"And this young lady is—I'm so sorry, dear, but I've forgotten your name," Shantal said.

"Majuna Chakraboti."

"Ah, yes, Majuna."

Now it was Majuna's turn to have her hand kissed. Naidu threw her a burning glance, saying, "So happy to meet *you*."

Majuna looked smug.

Carter cleared his throat. "Maybe you can answer a question that's bothering me," he said. "How can a train disappear?"

"That is a question that has been bothering us all, Mr. Webster," Naidu said. "Train four-two-nine does not answer its radio. It is now being looked for with search planes."

"I'm sure it's nothing more than a mechanical mishap," Shantal said.

"I hope so," Naidu said.

An operator tore off his headset and shouted, "They're coming in!"

The stationmaster, a burly, full-bearded man, hurried over. "Eh? What's that? Train four-two-nine is coming in?!"

"Yes! One of the search planes just spotted it on this side of Srithram Tunnel!"

"Are they stuck?"

"No, no, they're coming in!"

The harried personnel broke the tension with a loud, lusty cheer, but after a moment, relief was replaced with anger. The stationmaster thumped his fist on the desk so hard that the pencils flew off it.

"We'll be hours straightening out this mess! Those idiots had better have a damned good explanation, that's all I have to say!" he stormed.

"That certainly is a relief," Shantal Singh Sardar confided. "I was beginning to fear that the train had met with foul play. I could never forgive myself if anything happened to the brave doctors and nurses who have come to help us in our time of trouble."

"Shall we go out to the platform and meet them?" Naidu asked.

"They won't be here for a while yet. I'd like to stay out of the sun until they arrive."

"As you say, Shantal."

"The window over there faces west. We'll be able to see them coming," Shantal said.

The group drifted over to the big picture window.

A breathtaking vista lay spread out below. Vast golden plains stretched out to the horizon, shimmering in honeyed sunlight. The tracks of the line to Yatha Hunda arrowed across the great expanse, converging at the ranked blue-gray cones of the Srithram range.

After a time, a smudge of motion appeared on the tracks, hovering just at the edge of visibility. Quite a bit more time passed before the crawling blot resolved itself into a locomotive pulling some passenger cars and a caboose.

"Here it is at last!" Naidu said.

"Moving kind of slow, don't you think?" Carter noted.

"Quite."

Train 429 poked along at a snail's pace. At first, Carter was inclined to chalk it up to an illusion of distance, reasoning that the plains were so vast that the train only appeared to be moving so slowly.

As the minutes dragged on, with little forward progress on the part of the train, Carter realized that it looked like it was moving slowly because it *was* moving slowly. It rolled down the line with the velocity of cool molasses running uphill, and finally came to a dead stop a quarter mile outside Mhoti Station.

FIFTEEN

Train 429 out of Yatha Hunda arrived accompanied by an aerial escort, but not the search planes that had gone aloft to look for it. Their hunt ended, the planes had headed back to their base. Rather, the train was escorted by a flock of big black buzzards that soared on the thermals over the cars, making big wheels in the sky. One of them, bolder than the rest, fluttered to a landing on top of one of the passenger cars and perched there, preening.

There was no other movement. No sheepish engineers climbed out of the locomotive to offer their alibis for the delay. No passengers exited the long cars. No soldiers showed themselves. The train sat silent on the track.

When it first ground to a halt, the crowds thronging the station poured off the platforms, scrambling along the tracks to the train. Leading the pack were railway officials in a hurry to discover who was to blame for the foul-up. They were followed by a mass of friends and relatives of the passengers.

As the crowd neared the train, its unnatural stillness slowed them to a halt. At first, nobody noticed the words scrawled on the sides of the cars. Everyone was too busy wondering where the passengers were. Not a soul could be seen through the blank windows.

An officious constable shouldered his way through the still, silent crowd. Gravel crunched underfoot as he made his way to the train. As he neared it, he stopped, reeled, and gagged. He covered his face with a handkerchief and climbed on the train, entering a passenger car.

A moment later he staggered out, his face a mask of horror. "They're dead!"

"What?"

"They're dead, all dead!" He sat down between the tracks and started weeping.

The maharanee had more than Khaitan and Balindra to protect her. In all, twelve liveried, well-armed Djanjeri tribesmen formed her personal bodyguard. Now, in response to the emergency, they encircled their mistress. The tough tribesmen exuded vigilance and an air of deadly competence.

Shantal Singh Sardar shivered. "I can't look! Violence terrifies me!"

Ashwin Naidu held her hand in both of his, squeezing it.

Carter, Majuna, and Inspector Bhalk had already made their way to the front of the crowd, none of whose members were inclined to investigate. They seemed gripped by an almost supernatural fear. Again and again, individuals cried out a short, guttural phrase that held supreme significance, a cry taken up by more and more members of the crowd.

"What does that cry mean?" Carter asked.

"Death Train," Majuna said. "They're saying that the Death Train has returned."

There were phrases scrawled in dripping red on the sides of some of the cars, in letters three feet high. Fewer than a dozen bullet holes speckled the train, and two windows were shot out. Those were the only outward signs of violence.

When Carter neared the train, the stink hit him. It was so strong that it took all his self-control to keep from vomiting. The smell of death, mass death, aggravated by the punishing heat.

Covering his nose and mouth as best he could, he went forward. He made another discovery. The words scrawled on the train weren't written in red paint. They were written in blood.

"What do they say?" Carter asked.

" '*Khalistan murdabad*,' " Bhalk read, then he translated. "Death to Khalistan. This is bad, very bad."

The buzzard squawked at them as they mounted the stairs to the carriage. Carter paused on the top step, his attention caught by an ominous new development.

A group of about a hundred men had emerged from the slums north of Mhoti Station. They were turbaned Sikhs armed with swords, knives, and clubs, and they were making their way toward the train.

Inspector Bhalk muttered, "Very, very bad."

The trio entered the railway car.

Inspector Bhalk had been a child when the Death Trains first rolled, but they were a horror that once known, could never be forgotten. The nightmare was native to the troubled Punjab, and began in 1947 when the subcontinent was partitioned into the nations of Hindu India and Moslem Pakistan. The Punjab was split right down the middle, with half its territory going to Pakistan and half to India. The Moslems fled to

Pakistan, while the Sikh and Hindu refugees streamed toward India.

Both sides traveled by train, and that was when the Death Trains began to roll. Cars full of refugees were ambushed, their occupants slaughtered, and the trains were sent on down the track to arrive at their destination with a cargo of corpses.

The Death Trains.

Some forty years later, new hatreds and violence infected the state. The once allied Hindus and Sikhs of the Punjab were now at each other's throats. Many Sikhs had embraced the separatist dream of their own nation-state—Khalistan, the "Land of the Pure." The Hindus were no less fervent about remaining part of the Indian nation. This was the root cause of the violence that led to the Golden Temple Massacre, a violence now reaching new peaks.

The constable had been right. All the passengers were dead. They had been dead only a few hours, but already they were infested with fat black flies. The carriage floors were carpeted with corpses, their limbs intertwined like snakes. Many were frozen in contorted postures, their faces studies in agony, their flesh waxy and bloated. The majority showed superficial bleeding from the eyes, ears, nose, and mouth.

The cause of death was a mystery. The engineer, fireman, and some of the crew had been shot dead—no mystery there. But the others had died without a mark of violence on their bodies, save for minor injuries sustained in the course of convulsions. Even the platoon of army infantrymen had succumbed without a fight. But their weapons, ammunition, and gear were gone.

Bhalk's voice was muffled by the handkerchief held pressed to the lower half of his face. "It's not poison. I can think of no food or drink that would have been universally consumed by passengers in first and third classes alike."

"It's horrible," Majuna whispered. "Have you any idea what might have caused it?"

"I've got a theory," Carter said. "I'll tell you outside. I can't take the smell in here any more."

The trio stepped out onto the carriage platform. Among the crowd, mass grief was replaced by a more dangerous emotion—hate. And the mob of well-armed Sikhs from the slum, who had now joined the crowd, were doing their best to stoke the fires.

"It's funny how those characters showed up so fast," Carter said. "It's almost as if they'd had some advance notice."

Bhalk nodded. "I must agree. I suggest that we absent ourselves with all possible haste."

But the volatile mob had reached the flashpoint. The Sikhs in the crowd pointed to the messages written in blood on the sides of the train—*Khalistan murdabad* —death to Khalistan. Only the Hindus could have done such a thing, they shouted, because they were the ones opposed to the Land of the Pure.

The newly arrived gang of troublemakers shouted the loudest and the longest. They rattled their swords and daggers. They were the first to send up the cry:

"Kill the Hindus!"

The Hindus among the crowd were easily recognized, particularly the men who went beardless and without turbans. The scene boiled over into a screaming, shouting, murderous melee.

The Sikh gang from the slums didn't stop at punching and kicking and gouging. They wanted blood. A scream rang out and a bloody *kirpan* was brandished in triumph, announcing the first kill of a Hindu.

This was the signal for the rest of the gang to fall on the Hindus with a ferocity bred of fanaticism. Others, emboldened by the actions of their militant brothers, were quick to take up the cause. Their zeal was inflamed by the two-to-one odds in their favor. Butchery and slaughter broke out on every side.

Somebody reached up to the carriage platform and grabbed Carter's ankle. Carter's other foot came down hard, stomping the bones of the grabber's hand into jelly. The man let go and fell down, screaming.

A red-eyed Sikh *goondah* jumped up on the platform and grabbed Majuna, tearing her skirt. She slammed her knee between his legs, and followed up with a palm-heel strike to his nose, spreading it over half his face. He toppled back into the shouting mass of rioters. Their numbers were so thick that he was carried aloft on top of them for a moment before being dragged down underfoot and trampled.

But a dozen more surged forward to take his place. Only the press of numbers prevented them from over-whelming the train. Dozens of clawlike hands reached for them on either side. Majuna was a Hindu, Bhalk looked like one, and Carter was a foreign stranger and doubly detested.

"Let's get out of here!" Carter shouted.

A rioter grabbed Bhalk's legs and wouldn't let go. The little inspector stood there, his folder still tucked under his arm, fighting to kick free.

Carter moved to help him, but his attention was diverted by the wild thrust of a *kirpan* at his own legs. Carter jumped up, dodging the strike, then came down with a kick directly into the swordsman's face.

Majuna saw Bhalk being dragged down. "Inspector!" she cried. She reached for him, trying to hold him, but he was torn from her grasp and dragged off the platform.

"No!" Majuna shrieked.

"Bhalk! Bhalk!" Carter couldn't even see Bhalk any-more. The inspector had disappeared into the mass of rioters. "Bhalk!"

"We have to find him!" Majuna said. *"Inspector!"*

A wedge of blue-turbaned swordsmen forced their way toward the platform, bearing down on Carter and Majuna.

"Inspector!" Majuna kept shouting.

The attacker whose face Carter had kicked had dropped his *kirpan*, and the killmaster had snatched it up. He figured that might be better than a gun for getting through the crowd. His other hand grasped Majuna's wrist, pulling her back from where Bhalk had fallen. "We've got to save ourselves!"

Fanatics milled on both sides, flailing their knives and swords, screaming, "Kill, kill!"

There was one way out. Carter flung open the carriage door and pushed Majuna through it. "This way!"

Footsteps pounded on the platform. The door was kicked open by a Sikh with hatred in his eyes and a club in his hand. He started forward.

Suddenly there was a pistol in Majuna's hand. She shot him in the face and the bullet drilled through his eye to blow a hole in his skull.

Carter and Majuna moved down the aisle toward the rear of the car. It was a nightmare. There was no way to avoid stepping on the dead. Gunfire crackled outside, intermittent shots that did nothing to subdue the riot. Carter hoped that Corporal Vinobha and his squad were able to do something—or had called for reinforcements.

Finally, by walking from car to car to the end of the train, they reached a point where the mob was thinner. There they climbed down to the ground. A shrieking swordsman rushed them, *kirpan* raised high to deliver a murderous slash. But while he waved the sword wildly, Carter ran him through the belly. The Killmaster twisted his sword before pulling it out, its blade dripping bright red. The swordsman crumpled.

Wild violence engulfed Mhoti Station. The rioters had gone berserk, smashing windows and storming inside to massacre the non-Sikh station personnel. Torches came out and the building was set on fire.

"We can't go that way!" Carter panted. The area northwest of the station seemed the most promising direction. Carter glimpsed a road between two outbuildings. Where there was a road, there would be cars to commandeer. He and Majuna ran for it.

A handful of rioters took out after them.

It wasn't easy running flat out in that sweltering heat, but Carter and Majuna had a powerful incentive: survival. When they were about twenty yards from the road, Majuna tripped and fell, and their four pursuers shouted with triumph as they closed the distance.

Carter let go of the *kirpan* and yanked Wilhelmina from her holster. He put a bullet in each member of the quartet, killing them all before the sword hit the dust. They hit the ground a second later. Then he and Majuna made their way into a block of buildings and hurried down an alley to the street beyond. Excited people dashed to and fro, most of them heading in the opposite direction, toward the station. The excitement wasn't in this part of town. Yet.

But it was still a bad place to be: a few blocks to the east stood the slum from which the Sikh gang had come and mobs swarmed there.

"Where do we go now?" Majuna asked.

"Out of here," Carter said. "What we need is a car—wait a minute, look at this!"

Three cars cruised down the street in a convoy. The lead and tail cars were battered, serviceable vehicles filled with white-liveried Sikhs with guns. The car in the middle was a luxury sedan—a cloud-white Zimmer Golden Spirit convertible. Reflected light glimmered on its gold-plated hood ornament and hubcaps. More white-clad Sikhs clung to the sides of the car, perched on the running boards, holding rifles braced at the hip.

Rifle barrels bristled from the other two cars as well.

The three-car convoy drew abreast of them. Carter and Majuna hesitated, unsure of what to do next.

The convoy slowed to a halt. A woman stood up in the rear of the Zimmer.

"It's the maharanee!" Carter exclaimed.

Her men stepped down from the running boards and dismounted from the other cars. Shantal Singh Sardar waved at Carter, beckoning him.

Still, Carter hesitated. He looked behind him. The immediate vicinity was clear of rioters.

"What shall we do?" Majuna said.

"I don't know," Carter said. "But I've got a funny feeling that we're better off steering clear of her until we know where things stand."

Majuna nodded. "I don't trust her."

"I'll reserve judgment on that until later, but for now, let's make ourselves scarce."

They started to retreat into an alley.

A harsh voice bawled, "Halt!"

More persuasive than the barked command was the racketing sound of many rifle bolts slamming into place.

"Aw, shit," mumbled Carter.

He and Majuna turned around. Over a dozen rifles were trained on them.

"Well," Carter said, "at least now we know where we stand."

"Should we run for it?"

"That would be like trying to outrun a firing squad," Carter said. "I'd hate to give my good buddies Khaitan and Balindra an excuse to start blasting."

Balindra opened the rear door of the Golden Spirit, mockingly gesturing for the couple to enter.

Carter and Majuna crossed the road with leaden feet. The smiling maharanee sat in the back seat and waved to them. Tendrils of smoke from the burning terminal drifted into view.

"I was hoping we'd find you," Shantal Singh Sardar said.

"So was I," Khaitan said, smiling. His grin was a second scar slashing his face.

"I insist that you accept my protection. For your own good, of course," Shantal added.

Carter came forward easily, smiling as if he couldn't be more delighted to see her. He couldn't outrun bullets, but if he got close enough, he might be able to put Wilhelmina or Pierre into play.

"Well, if you insist . . . " the Killmaster said smoothly.

Khaitan smashed Carter with the butt of his rifle. The Killmaster said no more. He went down.

Inspector Bhalk knew a lot about riots. He'd seen demonstrations in Calcutta where the population of entire quarters had turned into a howling, screaming, blood-mad mob. Compared to that, the Mhoti Station outbreak seemed tame. But it could kill him just as surely as the big city riots he'd managed to survive.

When he knew that he was going to be pulled off the platform of the railroad car, Bhalk had stopped fighting it. Instead, he dived into the midst of the mob, and dived deep.

He was submerged in a flood tide of humanity. That was his best defense. So many people were trying to kill him that they got in each other's way.

At first, the close-packed rioters blocked his path, but Bhalk was agile, intent, and so thin that he was able to wriggle through the forest of legs surrounding him, running a gauntlet of blows and kicks. He reached his goal, rolled over the rail and under the train.

Howls of frustration arose from those who had tried

to kill him. They tried to reach him, but they were blocked by the random surges of the crowd.

Bhalk didn't linger to catch his breath. Still clutching his folder, he crawled over the ties and below the railroad cars, making for the front of the train.

Those who had seen him escape howled for his blood, but their pursuit was frustrated by the sheer weight of numbers. In seconds, Bhalk had left them behind. The rioters engulfing the rest of the train had no idea to that he was under there.

Finally he stopped under the last railway carriage before the engine. He stretched out between the rails and played dead while chaos reigned on either side. Murdered men and women fell around him, hideously mutilated and dismembered. Blood splashed on his suit, which helped him blend in with the corpses surrounding his body.

Shooting broke out, and the crowd thinned. The railroad station building itself had become the focal point of the violence.

Bhalk measured his chances, then scrambled out on the right side, putting the locomotive between him and the station. The bulk of the shooting came further down the track, to the east. Bhalk recognized the distinctive crackling of the rifles used by the Indian army. Corporal Vinobha and his squad were putting up some spirited resistance.

Bhalk could see the soldiers now, entrenched behind the thick stone blocks at the base of a water tower. Bodies sprawled around them. The rioters had now had enough of throwing themselves toward certain death by trying to storm the army barricade. Why attack armed soldiers when there were so many defenseless civilians around?

Bhalk didn't want to be shot by mistake, so he decided to work his way over carefully. Hunched low, folder tucked under his arm, he broke for cover.

At the station, Khaitan recognized Bhalk's white-suited figure. He sent three of his men after him. One asked, "Do we take him alive?"

Khaitan shook his head and drew his finger across his neck in a throat-slitting gesture. Laughing, the three Djanjeri tribesmen took off after Bhalk. They were big, powerful men in the peak of physical condition who could fight all day and carouse all night and not even work up a yawn. They raced after their prey, strong legs pounding, loping along, easily cutting the distance.

They could have shot him, but where was the fun in that?

Winded, Bhalk staggered into a space bounded by shacks. Too late, he realized it was a cul-de-sac, a dead end. But by that time, his pursuers had blocked his avenue of escape.

Bhalk stepped back. His foot hit a wall and he realized there was no place left to go.

The rasp of razor-sharp *kirpans* sliding out of their well-oiled scabbards was multiplied threefold as the tribesmen drew their swords. With smiles on their faces, they carved empty air as they closed in on the inspector.

Bhalk's right hand reached for the side vent of his folder. A thin slit stretched from its top to its bottom, and Bhalk thrust his hand inside the folder. Stuffed inside was a big .357 magnum revolver with a six-inch barrel.

Bhalk didn't bother to take the gun out of the folder. He squeezed the trigger three times, blasting through the folder, and blasting through the three tribesmen, too.

He shot each one in the chest, their blood immediately creating a crimson stain in the center of their fancy white tunics. He didn't need more than one shot for each of them.

And that was why Inspector Savatta Bhalk never went

anywhere without his well-worn folder.

Detouring around the bodies, Bhalk made his way to the water tower. He found some good cover, and called the name of Corporal Vinobha until he was heard during a lull in the shooting. He hadn't ran a gauntlet of enemies only to be shot by his allies at the finish.

"Hold your fire, men!" Corporal Vinobha shouted. "It's the inspector!"

Bhalk scrambled to safety behind their line.

SIXTEEN

"Wake up, Mr. Webster."

Carter was sprawled facedown on a stone floor. He didn't move.

Somebody splashed a bucket of warm, slimy water on him. He still didn't move.

"I'll rouse him," said a second voice. Booted footsteps approached. "Get up!"

Carter was kicked in the side. He didn't budge.

"I said, get up, dog!"

A second kick was launched, but it never reached its target. Carter moved.

The Killmaster rolled on his side just as Khaitan's foot began its kick. Carter crossed his wrists in an X-block, trapping the foot between his hands. Swiftly shifting his grip, Carter twisted the foot in a direction it wasn't designed to go.

Khaitan screamed.

The Sikh was precariously balanced on one leg, since Carter held the other off the floor. The Killmaster whipped his own leg across the stones, sweeping Khaitan's leg out from under him. Khaitan went flying, landing with a thud.

Carter got his feet under him, jumped up, and started for Khaitan to finish him off.

The sound of a dozen safeties being flipped off as many rifles halted him.

The first speaker sardonically applauded. "Bravo, Mr. Webster! Or, should I say—Mr. Nick Carter?"

"You can say what you please, Rogov," Carter said. "This time you've got the guns."

"There won't be another time for you, Killmaster."

Khaitan stood up, favoring the leg that Carter had twisted. Rage colored his face purple, making his crescent-shaped scar look dead white by comparison. He started forward.

Even with twelve guns pointed at him by the maharanee's white-uniformed Djanjeri guards, Carter wasn't going to stand and take it from Khaitan. He geared up to deliver a combination of lethal blows.

The big Sikh didn't know it, but he was reprieved from death when Shantal Singh Sardar snapped: "Khaitan! Stand aside and leave him alone!"

Absolute obedience warred with absolute rage in the tribesman. He stood torn by conflicting impulses, his heavy hands opening and closing, aching to tear into the stranger who had bested him not once, but twice.

"Khaitan!"

For generations, the commands of the maharajahs and maharanees of Samsirbad had been the word of God to the Djanjeri vassals who had pledged total loyalty to their lords and masters. Or, in this case, mistress.

Khaitan didn't back off, but he didn't keep coming.

Carter was grateful for the adrenaline that the clash sent pumping through his system. He still felt pretty terrible; the back of his skull was one enormous bruise. The pain was agonizing every time it throbbed, and it wouldn't stop throbbing.

The rest of him didn't feel much better. He felt as if he'd been worked over while he was knocked out. He probably had been. He was nauseated and a little dizzy, and hoped he wouldn't throw up.

He was naked, too.

He took a look around. He'd been coming to when he was dragged in there and unceremoniously dumped on the stone floor. He'd pretended to be in worse shape than he was, hoping it would lull his captors and give him the opening he needed to make a break.

He was in the throne room of what had to be the maharanee's palace in Samsirbad, west of Mhoti in the Srithram mountain range. It was a great vaulted stone hall, its groined, barrel-vaulted ceiling thick with shadows.

The vast chamber dwarfed its occupants. He stood in the middle of the room. At the far end was a raised dais topped by an elaborately carved wooden throne. Flanking it on either side were a pair of enormous ivory tusks, yellow with age, placed so they formed an arch over the chair.

Seated on the throne was Shantal Singh Sardar. Gone now was the fashionable dress and the Italian shoes. The maharanee was dressed in a brilliant red silk sari stiff with gold embroidery. The adornments she had worn earlier that day looked demure compared to the weight of gold and jewels now bedecking her from head to toe. Her small feet were shod in slippers encrusted with precious gems.

Standing at her right side, placed one step below the throne, was Ashwin Naidu. On her left, two steps down,

was Sergei Ivanovich Rogov and another Westerner
Carter didn't recognize but who fit the description
Vashti had given him of the accomplice who had been
with Rogov at the *kalighat*.

Ranked at right angles to the throne were two lines of
six Djanjeri tribesmen, all armed, and all of them training their weapons on Carter. Should he be so rash as to
rush the throne, they'd cut him down before he could
take more than a few paces.

Majuna was nowhere in sight.

The situation looked pretty grim. It got grimmer still
as Carter made a disheartening discovery. He realized
that his jaws ached brutally at their hinges; they felt as if
they'd been wrenched apart. Carter's probing tongue
encountered an unfamiliar gap in his back molars.

The hole had been formerly occupied by a poison pill,
the death capsule contained in a cleverly disguised
tooth. The poison pill was standard equipment for all
Killmasters and other AXE agents whose jobs took
them into danger. All one had to do was shove the jaws
at an unnatural angle and bite down hard on the hollow
tooth. Instant death would result, saving a captured
agent from the horrors of torture.

Carter's poison pill tooth was gone. Rogov knew that
trick too. No doubt he had something very much like it
as standard issue from his KGB bosses in the infamous
Department 8 of Directorate S, the Kremlin's number
one wrecking crew.

But Carter knew that if worst came to worst, he could
make them kill him. A bullet was a clean exit, at least. A
rush at the maharanee would provoke the guardsmen
into firing.

Carter approached the throne. The guardsmen followed him with their gun muzzles.

Shantal said, "Let him advance."

When Carter was within twenty feet of the throne,

Rogov said, "That's far enough, Killmaster."

Shantal turned on him, her agate eyes flashing. "I'll give the orders here! Never forget that!"

"A thousand pardons, Your Majesty," Rogov apologized with poor grace. "But you don't know how dangerous this man is! In fact, the smartest thing I could do right now is to put a bullet in his head." He reached for his pistol.

"Put your gun away, you fool!" Shantal barked. "You know how my Djanjeris are! They're liable to think you're threatening me, and if they do, that will be the end of you!"

The guardsmen didn't understand English, but they tensed when they saw Rogov's pistol. The maharanee reassured them with a few curt phrases, and they backed off, but they looked at Rogov as if measuring him for a grave.

"For heaven's sake, Rogov, don't be a bloody ass!" Lundy said. "You'll get both of us killed!"

"Shut up," Rogov hissed.

"I won't shut up. I've told you time and again that I don't take orders from you. We're equals, and don't you forget it!"

"*Shut up!*"

Lundy shut up. But Rogov put his gun away.

"Be still, the both of you!" Shantal said. "Your magpie chattering offends my ears!"

"You're right not to trust them," Carter said. "Rogov would sell his own mother down the river and I'm sure his pal would do the same. You'll have to watch to see that they don't sell *you* out, Maharanee."

"Divide and conquer," Rogov said with a sneer. "The oldest game in the book! Save your breath, Killmaster. You'll need it."

"That was a cute trick you pulled on the train today, Rogov," Carter said.

Rogov smiled. "You liked it? I'm rather proud of it myself. A new variation on a classic theme."

"I don't think your KGB bosses will appreciate the headlines when the world learns that a Soviet-made poison gas is being used on Punjabi citizens."

"Oh, you are clever!" Lundy said. "That's very good, really!"

Carter had known from the symptoms exhibited by the Death Train victims that a powerful poison gas had been used. He'd seen the same superficial bleeding from the orifices in the skull when he had been trapped behind the lines during the Vietnam War. The Soviet-backed Vietnamese had shelled Cambodian forces with canisters of the virulent poison gas whose polysyllabic classification had been shortened to Tri-Neuro-Disrupter, or TND.

TND was a complex molecule that killed its victims not by asphyxiation, but by shutting down their central nervous systems. The gas was colorless, odorless, and tasteless. Once inhaled by the victim, it passed through the mucous membranes and entered the bloodstream. TND molecules bound to neural receptors in the body, blocking them so they could not function. The result was that all the autonomic functions of the body shut down, like turning off a switch.

Its great advantage was that it had to be inhaled in order to act on the nerves. That meant that relatively untrained personnel could use it, so long as they wore simple gas masks.

"Headlines?" Rogov crowed. "There won't be any headlines. After tomorrow, nobody will even remember train four-two-nine."

"What happens tomorrow?" Carter said.

"I don't mind telling you, Carter, since you won't be here to see it. Pity, too. You'd appreciate the genius of it."

"Do tell."

"Tomorrow at noon, the prime minister is going to attend a very special ceremony at the Golden Temple in Amritsar. He's going to sign an agreement granting new autonomy and quasi-independence to the Punjab. Only he'll never get to sign it.

"The heroic freedom fighters of the Khalistan Commando Force will get him first. There's a secret passage under the shrine that nobody knows about but us, because we liquidated all unreliable persons who had the knowledge. That underground chamber will be loaded with canisters of TND. At the precise moment that the prime minister sets pen to paper, the gas will be released. And that will be it for the prime minister."

"Along with everybody else inside the Golden Temple," Carter added.

Rogov laughed. "I don't intend to be there myself."

"No. Knowing the way you operate, you'll be getting your tail as far away from Amritsar as possible."

Carter spoke to the maharanee. "In my country we have a word for characters who start fires and run away. We call them firebugs. And that's what Rogov is, a firebug. He'll reap the benefit, but you'll pay the price. You, and all the rest of your countrymen."

"I think not," Shantal said. "The prime minister's death will signal the dawn of the new age of Khalistan. A fitting revenge for the Golden Temple Massacre."

"What about your own people who will die with him?"

"They are not my people. Those who would trade with the oppressors of the proud Sikh nation deserve to die. At best they are cowards and appeasers. At one stroke, they will all be eliminated, ridding us of enemies from without and within."

"I don't have to look too far to see where the new leadership is going to come from."

"Exactly," Shantal said. "Oh, you are clever!"

"But you are not," Carter said. "Do you think India is going to let you assassinate their leader and secede? They'll cover the Punjab with troops, and with blood."

"Let them try, let them try. We Sikhs do not fear martyrdom for our holy cause. Are you as brave?"

"Let's find out," Rogov breathed. "Kill him!"

"What have you got planned for me, Maharanee?" Carter asked. "Something special, I'm sure."

"I regret that we did not meet under different circumstances," Shantal mused, looking at his body. "But today you are my enemy. You must die."

"You come from a warlike race. I claim the right to die a warrior's death," Carter said.

Rogov knew where Carter was heading and tried to keep him from getting there. "Claim? Rights? Strange language for a defeated foe! You deserve to die like a dog. And you shall."

Carter worked the needle: "Who's in charge here? You, Maharanee? Or this coward who's afraid to face me in single combat?"

"Shut your mouth, Carter," Rogov growled.

"Even in the throne room you give the orders, eh, Rogov?"

"You are going to die, Carter!"

"I'll keep a place in hell warm for you, Rogov."

"You'll have quite a wait, Killmaster. I don't intend to die for a long, long time."

"Who does?" Carter said. "Nobody here intends to die. But they will if they let themselves be used by you."

"That's enough!" Shantal said. "Be still, both of you!"

"You make a lot of noise for a man with no clothes on, Carter," Rogov said. "But it's nothing compared to the noise you'll make when I start tightening the screws!"

The maharanee was becoming annoyed. "Be silent, I command you!"

The guardsmen laid their hands on their swords. Lundy tugged at the Russian's sleeve, muttering out of the side of his mouth, "Good Lord, Rogov, stop provoking these savages! Sit down and shut up!"

The Russian eyed the angry guards, then sat down and shut up.

"You claim a warrior's death?" Shantal Singh Sardar said to Carter. "So be it. We shall see what you are made of."

SEVENTEEN

There had been a change in the weather. The air was heavy, oppressive, thick with moisture. The bowl of sky was a dull, leaden, yellow-gray color. A steadily increasing wind blew from the south, chasing streamers of clouds across the swollen face of the sulphurous sun sinking in the west.

"The day grows short," Khaitan said. "But it will outlive you, Yankee."

Carter didn't say anything. As Rogov had suggested, he was saving his breath. He was going to need it.

The ancestral home of the Singh Sardars had been built on a promontory some hundred feet above a winding loop of a tributary of the Sutlej River. Carter could hear but not see the waterway, which was hidden from sight by the thicket of forest running like a wall of green along the cliff's edge.

Behind him stood the maharanee's palace. She sat in one of its many pavilions, surrounded by exotic flowers. Joining her for the show were Ashwin Naidu, and Rogov and Lundy. Servants flanked the dignitaries, ceaselessly fanning the air with giant fans. The fans never stopped, but they were useless against the heavy air.

Immediately behind Carter were ten mounted horsemen, two riderless horses, and Khaitan and Balindra. Ahead of him stretched a few miles of tabletop plateau, gently rolling grassy meadows offering little in the way of cover.

To add insult to injury, Balindra had appropriated Hugo and Wilhelmina. The Luger was holstered at his hip, and the stiletto was stuck inside his red sash. Balindra had enjoyed poking and prodding Carter with his own gun, but that sport promised to pale beside the sport to come.

Balindra said something to Khaitan. Khaitan was only too happy to translate for the Killmaster:

"Balindra says you gave him a big stomachache before. He promises to return the favor—with this."

Carter knew that Khaitan was referring to the eight-foot lance brandished by Balindra. Khaitan had one, too, and so did each of the ten mounted men. The lances were used for the ancient blood sport of pig-sticking, a sport that remained enormously popular among the Djanjeri, especially when the "pig" was a two-legged foreign devil.

Carter paid no attention to their threats. This was his chance, the only one he'd have. His eyes were in constant motion, scanning the terrain, memorizing its features.

"A wild boar has been seen in the forest, but none of us has been able to catch him. I wonder if you'll be as lucky, American," Khaitan taunted.

But Carter knew that the Djanjeri weren't as good as they thought. With a little bit of luck, he could kill Khaitan and Balindra with his bare hands and feet, and maybe get his Luger back. But that wouldn't do him any good against the remaining ten tribesmen who sat impatiently on their horses, waiting for the game to begin. They all had pistols as well as lances. No, that wasn't the way to play it.

There was the flinty taste of dust in Carter's nose, the smell of horses, and the pungency of his own sweat. They had returned his trousers, but not his shoes. He felt the grass beneath his bare feet. It was crisp, sundried. Running on it wouldn't be much fun.

Horses moved nervously behind him. The mounted men talked among themselves in low, guttural voices punctuated by the occasional cruel laugh. Suddenly, a sharp, percussive tone rang out from the pavilion. A drummer was striking the taut skin head of a drum laying down an ominous, funereal beat.

"Here's something else for you to think about when you run, American," Khaitan said. "Balindra and I have an agreement. He gets your weapons, and I get your woman. After I run you through like the pig you are, I'm going to rape her and then kill her. What do you have to say about that?" Khaitan studied him with avid eyes, gauging his reaction.

"She's not my woman," Carter said evenly, "and I don't really care what happens to her. She's the one who got me into this mess."

Carter hoped that the turbaned tribesman believed his outrageous statement. It was a classic ploy of reverse psychology. The more Khaitan thought Carter cared about Majuna, the more pain he would cause her. Conversely, if he thought Carter didn't give a damn, punishing her might lose some of its appeal.

It looked as if the tactic might have worked. Khaitan

wasn't expecting Carter's reaction, and he didn't bother to hide his scowl of displeasure.

But the scowl was quickly replaced by the slash that passed for a smile on Khaitan's face, and the drumbeat began to increase its tempo.

The beat had started slower than a human heartbeat. Gradually it came faster and faster, and faster still, until it beat frantically—like the heart of a man in mortal terror.

"When the drum stops—run!" Khaitan said.

Khaitan and Balindra swung into their saddles. Carter shook out his arms and legs, loosening them up. His guts were churning; the waiting was always the worst. It would almost be a relief to get on with it.

The Djanjeri wanted sport, but not too much of it. They would give the prey a head start, but the Killmaster knew that it would be just enough to make things interesting, not enough to give him a fighting chance.

Or so they thought.

The drumbeats were now a relentless tattoo that rattled inside his head. He didn't bother to look behind him. In his mind's eye he saw the maharanee, sitting among her tropical blooms, cupping her determined chin in one hand, leaning forward with fascination as if she were wrapped up in a particularly engrossing chess problem.

He could visualize Rogov, too. The Russian didn't like this turn of events. He wasn't a sportsman, he was a professional, and he knew, he *knew*, that the best course of action would be to stop this tomfoolery and put a bullet through Carter's head. Lundy had had his hands full keeping Rogov from irritating his hosts with his insistent demands that Carter be liquidated at once.

And Majuna? Carter tried not to think about her. He hadn't inquired about her well-being for the same reason that he had faked indifference and resentment to

Khaitan. A show of concern on his part would be the surest way to guarantee her an unpleasant fate.

His thoughts whirled like a spinning top, whipped into a blur of motion by the drum.

Suddenly there was silence.

The drumming had stopped.

Carter started running.

He didn't sprint, he jogged, and only enough to make it look good. He waved his arms around a lot so it would appear as if he were putting out his maximum effort.

Carter did have one thing going for him: years of martial arts training in the AXE dojo had built up a thick layer of protective calluses on his feet. But they couldn't stand much of this terrain.

The air was so thick and heavy that jogging through it was like running through a huge steam bath. He hadn't gone more than twenty yards before his body was glistening with sweat. He felt as if he were having one of those awful nightmares where survival depends on speed but the dreamer is stalled in agonizing slow motion.

The drumming resumed. It would follow the same rhythmic progression as before, going from slow to fast, and when it reached a crescendo, the game would really begin.

Only this time the drummer was being stingy with the slow build-up, cutting it to a minimum.

Carter loped along, synchronizing his breath with his strides, finding a comfortable rhythm. His head start was a help; it greased stiff muscles and worked new flexibility into them. But he knew his solo run wouldn't last much longer.

The drumming stopped.

Hooves pounded the hard-baked ground as the twelve horsemen spurred their mounts forward. Carter let them get closer before glancing over his shoulder. The horses were cutting the distance fast!

He thought he knew how they were going to play it. They would stretch the fun for as long as possible, harrying him, jabbing, letting a little bit of life out of him at a time.

He glanced back again. The riders had cut the distance in half and were coming on fast. The Djanjeri were born horsemen. They were a tribe of centaurs, half man, half horse, coming at him in a row with lances extended. When he looked back, he put fear in his face to satisfy them, but could they see his expression? Their faces were blurs to him.

Only an idiot or a world-class runner would think he could outrace a horse, and Carter was neither. He was a fighter, not a runner. The time to make his play was as soon as possible, while he still had reserves of strength to draw on.

He could hear hoofbeats close behind him. Carter stopped running and pivoted to face them.

He made quite a picture: a sweat-soaked barefoot runner about to be mowed down by a dozen hard-riding horses. The setting sun gave the lances a yellowish gleam. The riders at the flanks of the line spread outward, forming a pincer movement to ensnare him.

A single lancer was about to run him down. At the last second, before the lance blade could score, Carter moved to the side. He did it with deliberate clumsiness, making it look like a lucky break instead of the skillful move it was.

Clods of dirt were kicked up by the horse's hooves, pelting him. Another horseman came at him. This time, Carter was lucky. The lance missed him, but the rider came so close that his horse's sweaty flank brushed Carter. Carter had never been a great fan of bullfights, and he never expected to be in the arena himself, tormented by Djanjeri picadors.

The riders wheeled their horses around to make another pass. Their goal was to form a circle around him so they could prick and jab at their leisure, and they all vied for the honor of drawing the first blood.

But Carter would draw it first. He knew he had to act fast; he was already winded from dodging the succession of rushing passes as rider after rider tried to spear him.

A tribesman on a gray stallion saw an opening and spurred his mount toward Carter. He held his lance low, in his right hand. Carter stood on the rider's right.

None of the Djanjeri went for a killing stroke. They aimed for his arms and legs, hoping to wound him, to weaken him. This rider was coming at him, looking to score on Carter's legs.

Another rider bore down from the opposite direction. A squeeze play.

At the final instant, Carter leaped to his right, darting almost under the animal's nose. His move put him on the stallion's left side. It was too late for the rider to switch his lance to the left.

As he passed by, Carter grabbed the lancer's left leg and held on tight. The horse kept going. The rider didn't.

The tribesman screamed as he fell off his horse. He landed on his neck and stopped screaming.

Carter knew there wasn't time for him to get the dead man's gun, not with the other rider almost on top of him, but he managed to snatch up the lance.

The charging Indian knew that the game was over and that this was for real. He, too, held his lance on the right as he came in riding low in the saddle, leaning far forward, reaching for the killing stroke.

This time, however, Carter didn't dodge to the horse's left. Timing his move, he got his lance inside the other's, parrying it to the side. He parried, then he planted the lance right in the rider's belly.

Carter's lance splintered, snapping in two. The half with the blade went through the rider's chest and out his back, its penetration aided by his own momentum. The rider was flung off his mount. The animal, frightened and confused, reared up on its hind legs, forelegs pawing the air.

Carter threw his arms around the horse's neck and swung himself up into the saddle. He kicked the horse's flanks with his feet, and the animal leaped forward with the Killmaster astride it.

The fun was over. The remaining horsemen got serious. With all their souls, they dreaded the maharanee's wrath if this man should escape.

Carter leaned far forward on his mount, his thighs pressing the horse's heaving flanks. He snatched up the trailing reins and kicked his heels into the animal, urging it to greater speed.

Khaitan's fury was boundless, and his reactions quick. He let go of his lance, clawed his pistol from its holster, and fired at the Killmaster as he gave chase. The rest of the Djanjeris followed his example, and gunfire erupted on the plateau.

Bullets whizzed in the air around Carter. Hitting a moving target with a pistol fired on horseback is no easy feat, but the Djanjeri lived by the gun, and Carter found some of their shots too close for comfort.

Suddenly there was a flat thwacking sound, an impact more felt than heard. The horse had been hit. The frightened, pain-crazed animal hurtled into a gallop.

The horse was bleeding, losing strength with every beat of its gallant heart. That killed Carter's plan to outride the hunters. And it could get him killed as well, he knew.

The edge of the cliff was on his left as he rode south. Through gaps in the trees he saw the river.

The Djanjeri were closing in fast. Carter abruptly swung his mount to the left, toward the line of the trees. The animal faltered, nearly losing its footing. The sheltering cover neared, but so did the tribesmen.

He was about a hundred feet from the thicket when the horse gave out. Its forelegs folded and it pitched forward with a piteous cry. Carter leaped clear of the saddle just in time to keep from being pinned under the beast.

He hit the ground rolling, absorbing the impact on his shoulders, keeping his head tucked down. The art of proper falling was one that was taught by the judo *sensei*s working for AXE, and Carter was an apt pupil.

Carter came out of his roll running. He was bruised and scratched, but his brief ride had given him the opportunity to catch his breath.

Thundering hooves approached. Bullets whined overhead, cutting leaves off branches. Carter threw some random zigs and zags into his forward motion, slowing him down but disrupting the riders' aim.

There was the brush, a solid wall of tangled undergrowth wrapping the thicket of trees. Carter spotted a gap in the foliage and dived in headfirst.

And not a second too soon. The bleeding soles of his feet were pelted by clods of dirt kicked up as the riders abruptly reined their horses to a halt and dismounted.

The undergrowth was not as impenetrable as it looked from the outside. Carter found that it was laced with narrow game trails. Keeping low, he wriggled under a tangle of thorn bushes.

"Go in there and get him! Don't let him escape!" Khaitan screamed.

The guardsmen plunged into the brush with drawn guns, fanning out, beating the bushes. They were at a disadvantage since they walked up high on two legs while Carter was at ground level crawling on his belly.

He came out of the thorn bushes into a glade, and dashed across it.

"There he is!" somebody yelled. A bullet blasted into a tree trunk a few inches above Carter's head, spraying him with bark and sap.

A thin trail opened that went deeper into the woods. Carter's bare feet pounded on the hard earth. The trail dipped into a hollow. A cluster of boulders were jumbled together, forming a cleft, a burrow big enough to hide a man.

Carter tore some leafy branches off a tree. If he hid in the hole and covered it with the branches, he might be able to elude capture. He could lie low until nightfall.

Guardsmen crashed through the brush on either side of him, beating the bushes to flush him out. Khaitan's booming voice predominated, screaming in Punjabi at his men. The scar-faced Sikh was whipping some methodical order into the search.

Carter hunkered down near the cleft in the rock. A meaty, gamy odor wafted out. Snufflings and snortings sounded in the burrow as a pair of blood-red eyes glared out at Carter.

The burrow was already occupied.

The rustle of leaves sounded only a few feet away. Carter edged away from the burrow, then dived behind a fallen tree just as a guardsman crashed into the hollow.

This guardsman had a thin, pinched face with close-set eyes and jutting cheekbones. He must have fancied himself as some kind of tracker. His face took on a shrewd expression as he saw fresh human footprints in the softer soil of the clearing.

A nearby comrade called his name. "Kushwant!"

Kushwant caught the other's eye and signaled him to silence. Smiling slyly, he put a finger to his lips. He pointed to the hole in the rocks, again motioning for silence.

Kushwant approached the burrow from the side, getting down on one knee. Suddenly, he crouched down in front of the hole, covering it with his gun.

"I've got him!" he crowed. "He's in here!"

Other guardsmen hurried toward the hollow. Kushwant motioned menacingly with his gun. "Come out of there, you! No tricks, or I'll shoot! You heard me! Come out—

"Yaaaaaaaaahhh!"

Out of the burrow hurtled a big, bristly, razor-tusked wild boar. The 250-pound animal was irked, and wasted no time in letting Kushwant know it. It came charging out, jaws gaping, wickedly upcurved tusks dripping hot, steaming saliva.

It ran over Kushwant, trampling him underfoot with its sharp hooves. It dug its snout into his middle, savaging the guard with its tusks, ripping him open while the struggling man's screams filled the air.

The other tribesmen followed his blood-curdling shrieks to the hollow, and stopped short at the grisly scene. Kushwant was finished, gutted. But he wasn't dead yet. His groans of mortal agony were mingled with the tusker's snortings and gruntings.

At first the men were too stunned to do anything. Instinctively, they held their fire for fear of hitting Kushwant, but it would have been a mercy if they had.

Through with Kushwant, the boar charged the nearest Djanjeri, bits of flesh dangling from its bloody snout.

Its bristly gray-brown hide was marked with many old wounds, some from lances wielded by men on horseback. If the concept of revenge could be part of a beast's consciousness, then it burned in that boar. The hated two-legged things had blundered into its territory, and he was very angry!

The next guardsman under attack jerked the trigger of his gun, pumping a slug into the animal. The bullet didn't have much effect, for the boar went for his legs.

A single slash of a yellow tusk opened up a leg from knee to crotch, severing the femoral artery.

The guardsman toppled and the boar trampled him. The boar wasn't going to wait for him to bleed to death. Its mouth opened wide, allowing the guardsman to look down its throat before its jaws closed on the hapless man's face.

Carter silently congratulated the boar as he slipped out of the hollow. He'd decided that this was his chance to clear out.

Mud mixed with blood covered the floor of the hollow. The Djanjeri emptied their pistols into the boar. One guard delivered the coup de grace to the mutilated guardsman. Soon the hollow was silent.

By then, Carter had put some distance between himself and the scene of the slaughter. He had gotten a break when he needed it most, but his luck was about to turn bad again.

First, he made the unhappy discovery that the grove in which he had hoped to find cover was an isolated island of vegetation, and not a particularly extensive one at that.

Then, Khaitan took a shot at him. And he used a rifle rather than a pistol. One of his men had carried the weapon in a saddle scabbard, and Khaitan had gone to get it while the boar savaged his comrades. It was a big-bore hunting rifle and could have finished the tusker with one well-placed shot, but Khaitan was after bigger game.

He took up a position at the edge of the trees. From his vantage point he covered the horses and the open ground that lay between the grove where he stood and the next.

A long blur of motion dashed between two trees.

Khaitan squeezed off a shot at Carter a split second too late. Carter was stung by wood chips scattered by the slug.

Khaitan fired twice more in Carter's general direction. He didn't expect the shots to hit Carter, but he wanted to signal his men. If he got lucky and tagged Carter, so much the better.

The boar had left two dead. Carter had accounted for two more. The odds against him were dropping, but not fast enough. And Khaitan was making things hotter with that big-game rifle.

Carter crouched in the bushes growing along the cliff's edge. The river lay some seventy-five feet below the sheer rock face, deep, turbulent, and swift-running. White water boiled around jagged rocks that loomed menacingly in the gathering dusk. It was a long way down.

Cover was minimal. Even as Carter searched for a hiding place, Khaitan burst from the nearby grove, rifle in hand. He saw Carter before Carter had a chance to duck.

"Here! Over here! Don't let him get away!"

Khaitan's men came running. The Djanjeri were inured to death and suffering, especially someone else's. The horror of the rampaging wild boar paled beside the fear of their own fates if Carter should escape.

Carter stood up.

Khaitan, surprised, thought he was surrendering. All sorts of scenarios of degradation, torture, and mutilation flashed through his mind, dizzying him with the possibilities.

Carter turned and jumped off the cliff.

Khaitan fired a shot at him anyway, but it just whistled through empty air. Carter had dropped out of sight.

In the split second before he took the plunge, Carter chose as his jumping-off point a ledge that leaned out over a deep section seemingly free and clear of large rocks. There was always the chance that rocks lay just below the surface, but he knew he didn't have much choice.

With the river he had a chance, however slim. With Khaitan and the rest of his buddies, he had no chance at all.

Carter jumped as far as he could. He fell straight down, legs together, toes pointed. The surface of the river looked as solid as concrete. He plummeted so quickly that there was no time to even form a thought.

He hit the dark water and went down, down, down. He felt a terrific sense of headlong rushing motion, and his arms felt as if they had been torn from their sockets.

Something battered his side, buffeting him so that he turned cartwheels underwater. The powerful current tossed him willy-nilly. . . .

Khaitan and his men gathered at the edge of the cliff, scanning the river. One of the guardsmen got excited and cried out, "I see him!"

"Where? Where?"

"Uh, no, it's just a rock," the man said sheepishly.

Khaitan cuffed him with a sizzling backhand that knocked him over.

"The American was shot," he told the others, matter-of-factly. "A mortal wound. He fell off the cliff into the river, dead. That is what we will tell the maharanee."

Shantal believed them, when they finally rode back and told her. But Rogov didn't. The Russian knew Carter a little better than Shantal did. He and Lundy left for Amritsar as soon as they could

So did the Djanjeri tribesmen charged with the awesome responsibility of unleashing the poison gas at the Golden Temple at noon on the following day.

EIGHTEEN

Few places are lonelier than the forgotten graveyards of yesterday's conquerors. Few graveyards were as forgotten as the one situated on a gentle knoll overlooking a shallow cove a few miles down the river from the ancestral home of the Singh Sardars.

A solitary jackal prowled among the shattered mausoleums, overturned headstones, and broken monuments. It kept its nose close to the weed-choked ground, sniffing for the scent of food.

Something splashed on its head. It looked up, its yellow eyes glimmering, shedding their own pale light in the dark, overcast night. The jackal scented rain, and sure enough, another drop splashed on its flanks.

Then it caught the scent of something else—something alive. It shied away from the scent. If the creature were dead, carrion, it would have been a delicacy. But the creature lived.

The jackal laughed. Its laugh was a weird sound, somewhere between a cough, a snort, and a barking wheeze.

That laugh was one of the sweetest sounds that Nick Carter had ever heard. Because hearing it meant that he was alive.

Battered and tumbled by the powerful current, the Killmaster had been flung more than a mile downstream before he was able to break loose from it. By swimming diagonally with the current, he had finally freed himself from the river's sucking grip, lurching ashore at this quiet cove. He had dragged himself into a place of concealment and collapsed.

Now he was awake and it was night. Carter took stock of himself. No broken bones, no internal injuries. He considered himself very lucky.

He was nearly naked and weaponless, but he was alive.

A strong wind swirled through the graveyard, chasing leaves and dried grasses around the markers of Englishmen who'd come a long, long way from home to die in India. Carter mused that he'd almost joined them.

He sat up with his back propped against a tilted headstone, savoring the breeze and the light drizzle misting on his face. His eyes took in the many ruined and toppled monuments. Finally, when he felt fully rested, he got up and walked back to the water. Carter waded hip-deep into the placid waters of the cove, looking up and down the river. He recognized landmarks to the north. He realized he wasn't too many miles from the maharanee's palace, and he started toward it.

While he walked toward it, his brain raced, working on a plan. Sneak up to the palace, kill a guard, take his clothes and weapon. Go inside, get more weapons, kill more men.

And one woman: the maharanee Shantal Singh Sardar.

He had to rescue Majuna—if she were still alive—get word to the authorities in Amritsar about the plot to assassinate the prime minister.

Oh, yes. Balindra had some things that belonged to Carter. He'd have to reclaim Wilhelmina and Hugo.

Carter reached the plateau. He skirted the edge of the woods, using them for cover as he approached. The misty drizzle was like fog, blurring lights into soft-focus hazes, obscuring visibility. The rain was his ally.

Carter was still some distance from the palace when he first noticed the surreptitious activity going on around it. He scrutinized it from a hiding place until he was sure of what he saw. His thoughts were still a bit fuzzy from the fall. It took him some time to put things together, but there was no mistaking what was going on.

A cordon of soldiers was surrounding the palace. Commandos in battle fatigues, heavily armed. Scores of them, hundreds perhaps, ringing the palace with automatic rifles, machine guns, mortars, the works.

The Indian army had arrived.

Carter thought about sitting this one out and watching the other guys fight. But he couldn't stay put; there was a massacre scheduled to take place in twelve hours and he had to stop it. A military unit would have communications equipment—field telephones and radios. He could get a message to Amritsar.

Carter strolled into plain view to surrender himself to the first soldiers he found. He had something going for him: the sight of a half-dressed American strolling across the plains of Samsirbad at midnight was so bizarre that the soldiers were too flabbergasted to do anything but stare in amazement.

But it was Carter's turn to stare in amazement some time later, when he was finally escorted to the commanding officers mapping out their final plan of attack on the palace.

Salted among the military men was a familiar face he

hadn't expected to see again.

"Inspector Bhalk!" Carter said with a huge grin. "I thought you were dead!"

"And I, you," Bhalk said, equally pleased that such was not the case. "Apparently the reports of both our deaths were mistaken!"

It didn't take much to make Carter feel like a new man. A set of battle fatigues, a couple of sandwiches, a few mugs of steaming tea liberally laced with brandy, and he felt like his old self again.

While Carter fortified the inner man, Inspector Bhalk briefed him on what had happened since their separation at Mhoti Station.

Joining up with Corporal Vinobha and his squad, Bhalk and the soldiers had survived the station riot. In the aftermath, Bhalk discovered eyewitnesses who had seen Carter and Majuna abducted by the maharanee's men. This was the smoking pistol, the fatal clue that linked Shantal Singh Sardar with the violence shaking the Punjab.

Bhalk had linked up with the commanding officers of the Indian army unit sent to Mhoti to quell the insurrection. Once the skeptical military men had verified his credentials with higher-ups in Delhi, they extended the full and complete cooperation with the inspector that the prime minister had mandated.

A hand-picked team of rugged Gurkha tribesmen, some of the fiercest fighting men in the world, had been rushed to Samsirbad to serve at Bhalk's direction. Ever since sundown, they had carefully infiltrated the area, readying for the strike.

"And then you came along," Bhalk concluded, "more dead than alive, holding the secret of the plot to murder the prime minister. Really, Mr. Carter, you are an astonishing fellow!"

"I could say the same about you, Inspector," Carter said, "and I think I will!"

"Your information about the palace defenses will prove invaluable," Bhalk said.

Carter drained his cup of tea and stood up. "This is one party I don't intend to miss, Inspector."

"The good captain informs me that the big show is ready to commence. Before we go, I have something that belongs to you. I'm afraid I was unable to salvage your suitcase, but I did save this," Bhalk said, handing Carter his duffel bag.

Carter unzipped the bag and took out the Power-Slam crossbow. "I can't thank you enough, Inspector," he said. "This may come in handy."

The captain strolled into view. "Ready whenever you are, Inspector."

"Right away, Captain."

The captain said, "You'll be joining our strike force, Mr. Carter?"

"Captain, I wouldn't miss it for the world!"

Balindra hated sentry duty. Still, manning a post on the palace's southern pavilion overlooking the gardens was far better than crawling around tunnels under the Golden Temple with a load of poison gas.

He hated this stinking rain, too. He spent as much of his night watch as possible sheltering under an overhanging parapet, playing with his new toys.

Balindra had never had a gun like the 9mm Luger. He stuck it in the top of his red sash and practiced his fast draw. Perhaps the rain made the grips slippery, but the pistol just didn't seem to want to stay in his hand. He'd nearly dropped it a half-dozen times. Once, the safety catch flipped off—he didn't know how—and he nearly shot himself in the foot with it.

Through sheets of rain, he sensed more than saw movement in the garden. Jackals? Not another boar, he prayed. He shuddered at the memory of what had happened in the hollow. Then he realized that the rustling in the perfumed garden was caused by men, dozens of them, rushing the palace.

Before he could give the alarm, somebody whistled behind his back. Reflexively, Balindra turned.

A crossbow bolt entered his belly to make the acquaintance of his spine.

The Killmaster eased out of the shadows where he'd been lurking, stepping swiftly across the pavilion. He went down on one knee, stripping Wilhelmina and Hugo from the dead Djanjeri. Carter wiped Wilhelmina dry before dropping her in the side-arm holster of his web belt. She wouldn't be staying there very long. There was work to do.

He went to the edge of the pavilion and signaled to the Gurkha commandos to advance.

"Don't shoot! I surrender!"

Maybe Ashwin Naidu was a coward, or maybe he just had good sense. But whatever the reason, he was one of the handful of Shantal Singh Sardar's followers to survive the raid on the palace.

It was all over but the mopping up. The struggle had been fast and furious. The palace was undermanned, due to the special squad that had gone to Amritsar. The Djanjeri defenders were brave to the point of foolhardiness, but they'd been overwhelmed by the sheer weight of numbers of the ferocious Gurkhas. Now the dead and dying lay everywhere.

The smell of cordite filled the air. The palace was a shambles, pockmarked with hundreds of bullet holes and cratered with scores of blast marks from the fragmentation grenades used when the fighting got really tough.

"Throw down your weapons and come out with your hands up!" someone shouted at Ashwin Naidu.

He didn't have weapons, but he had something better: lives. He emerged from the door leading down to the palace dungeons with the handful of people who'd been imprisoned by the maharanee.

One of them was Majuna Chakraboti.

She couldn't believe her eyes when she saw Inspector Bhalk and Nick Carter standing side by side, smoking guns still held in their hands. She rushed to them and embraced both men.

"I was lucky," Majuna told them. "Khaitan had to rush away to Amritsar before he had time to have his fun with me. The bastard promised to save me for his return and threw me in a cell."

As he was being led away, Ashwin Naidu insisted, "The maharanee commanded me to kill the prisoners when you attacked. I swore I would do it, but I didn't!"

Inspector Bhalk said, "I will make sure that your act of forbearance is brought to the attention of the magistrate in charge of your trial for treason, insurrection, and murder. Take him away!"

Naidu was taken away.

"Where is the maharanee?" Carter asked the inspector.

"A very good question," Bhalk replied. "I suggest we go upstairs, where her private quarters are located."

They started up the winding marble staircase, only to halt halfway up as Shantal Singh Sardar came into view.

"Look out!" somebody shouted. "She's got a gun!"

Carter lifted his Luger, and all eyes were riveted on the figure at the head of the stairs. No one made a sound or said a word.

Shantal Singh Sardar looked every inch a queen. She wore a diamond tiara, masses of jewelry, and a white silk sari shot through with gold and silver threads. She stood at the top of the stairway, holding a pistol in one hand and a jar of something in the other.

A wan smile curved her lips when she saw Carter.

"Rogov was right. I should have given you a bullet in the brain. Instead, I'll be taking it myself."

Shantal upended the jar over her head, pouring its contents over herself. It was oil, the sort used in lamps, and she soaked herself from head to toe.

Shantal said to Carter, "I told you I was not afraid of martyrdom."

She pressed the pistol muzzle under her left breast and squeezed the trigger. The shot was muffled.

Holding the gun at that point-blank range scorched her garments and flesh. The sparks ignited the oil-soaked fabric, and flames spread from head to toe in the span of a few heartbeats. In seconds, she was a human torch. The stairway became her funeral pyre. Her charred, blackened remains lay on the marble steps.

Suttee, the ancient custom that demanded that the new widow throw herself on the funeral pyre of her deceased husband as his body was being cremated, has long been outlawed in India.

Shantal Singh Sardar had no husband, but she was married to a dream, the mad dream of Khalistan, the Land of the Pure where she would hold absolute power as her ancestors once had.

That dream was dead, and the maharanee had not cared to outlive it.

NINETEEN

It was raining in Amritsar early the following morning, and trouble seemed imminent. Archdale Lundy had had enough of both. He could beat the rain by leaving the Punjab, and he was working on solving his troubles. That was why he had paid to bring to this city the three travelers from Delhi who were now breakfasting with him in the privacy of a cheap hotel room.

Trust was everything in his business, and he could no longer trust Rogov. The onetime highly professional agent had degenerated into an emotional, unpredictable hothead.

Right now, a gang of Djanjeri fanatics was crawling around in the sewers under the Golden Temple, intent on their deadly mission. By noon, they would have accomplished the crime of the century—or so Lundy liked to think of it.

Rogov was unreliable. Rogov could connect him with

the crime. He could connect Rogov to the crime. Lundy figured he'd better get rid of Rogov before Rogov got rid of him.

He sipped his tea and congratulated himself on his cleverness. The solution to the Rogov problem sat with him at the breakfast table, a three-part solution: a scrawny man, a fat woman, and an ancient fellow with a hideously scratched face.

Lundy slid a folded sheet of paper across the table. "It's all in there. That's where you'll find him. He's the one you want, the man who masterminded the slaughter at the *kalighat*."

None of the trio reached for the paper. They all just sat there, intently studying him.

Lundy pursed his lips, aware of a bitter taste in his mouth. There was something odd about the tea, he realized. The last thing he saw before he passed out, slumping over the table, were his three companions' untouched cups.

The scrawny man took out a golden cord and wrapped it around Lundy's neck and squeezed it until he was dead.

It was nothing personal. The Thugs just thought that Lundy was unreliable. They agreed to delay eating the sacred Goor until they strangled the other man, Lundy's associate, Rogov.

Primala picked up the piece of paper containing Rogov's address and put it in her purse.

Another trio made some last-minute preparations in a sewer tunnel below Amritsar. Carter, Majuna, and Inspector Bhalk finished rigging the plastique to a slimy stone wall.

They wore black wet suits and hardhats with miner's lamps. It had rained steadily all night and the waters were rising fast. The black current pouring through the tunnel reached up to their ankles.

Carter double-checked the fastenings securing the remote-controlled bomb to the tunnel wall; they were attached correctly. The wall vibrated with constant singing tension. On its other side was a feeder pipe ten feet in diameter that carried hundreds of gallons of river water every minute.

The tunnel they were in sloped downward to the secret passage going under the Darbar Sahib, the Sikhs' Golden Temple. Ashwin Naidu had been only too helpful in spilling his guts of everything he knew about the plot.

Carter, Majuna, and Bhalk had passed their own private verdict on the conspirators, and the sentence was death.

"I regret this," Inspector Bhalk said as he stowed away his waterproofed plans of the city sewer system. "But it is for the best. There must be no prisoners, no holy martyrs to further inflame the violent Khalistani separatists."

Carter didn't regret it; in this case he firmly believed that those who lived by the sword should die by it. The violence and hatred had to end. His only regret was that he wouldn't see the look on Khaitan's face when the wall was blown open, sending a river surging down the tunnel to flood the secret passage. Best of all, the TND gas was water soluble and would be rendered harmless by the flood.

The bomb was equipped with a remote-controlled detonator. When Carter pressed the button on his mini-transmitter, it would generate a high-frequency radio impulse that would activate the detonator.

Carter checked the bomb on the wall one last time. "Okay, let's get out of here—fast!"

A dull concussion reverberated through the cramped

confines of a tunnel crowded with a team of Djanjeri assassins laden with canisters of TND poison gas.

Long ago, the secret passage had been constructed as a bolt-hole for clandestine escape in case of siege. But it could serve as an entrance as well as an exit.

It was about to serve as a death chamber for the twenty-man team led by Khaitan.

The tunnel was too low to permit them to walk upright and too narrow to allow them to proceed in any way but single file. The mountain tribesmen were well disciplined, but they chafed at the claustrophobic confinement.

Adding to their discomfort were the gas masks they had worn from the moment they entered the tunnel. It was for their own protection in case someone accidentally unsealed one of the TND canisters.

Khaitan was edgy. He had been unable to contact the maharanee since his team left Samsirbad the previous evening. The cramped surroundings, the stifling gas mask, the deadly gas, even a superstitious awe of the Golden Temple—all worked on his normally iron nerves.

His men were in worse shape. Much worse. And when they heard that dull but powerful booming noise coming from somewhere higher up in the tunnel, they reached the breaking point.

Khaitan was in the lead. He turned around so he could face his men and whip them into line.

"What was that noise?" one of the guards said.

Khaitan laughed. "Are you men, or women in skirts? It's nothing, only an echo from the street."

Somebody insisted, "No, wait! I hear something!"

"Yes, I hear it too!"

Khaitan opened his mouth to give the guards hell. Since he had turned around to face them, he was the first to see a wall of fluid darkness thundering down the tunnel.

The surging flood slammed into the men with the force of a runaway express train. Above them, the hundreds of Sikhs and Hindus who thronged the sacred shrine to pray and work for an elusive peace didn't hear a thing.

It was not until the night of the following day that the Amritsar police notified Inspector Bhalk of a most bizarre case of multiple murder. When he learned the particulars of the crime, the inspector arranged for Nick Carter to visit the scene of the crime with him.

The killings—or killing and suicides—had taken place in a shabby hotel in a run-down section of the city. The bodies had been dead for over twenty-four hours, but the crime had not been discovered until recently. The officer in charge assured Bhalk that nothing had been tampered with.

Carter and Bhalk walked into the hotel room. Sergei Ivanovich Rogov lay sprawled on the floor with a golden cord deeply embedded in his neck. He had been strangled. With him were three more corpses, victims not of strangulation but of poisoning.

They were an enormously obese woman, an old man with a badly mangled left cheek, and a scrawny, middle-aged man. None carried any identification.

Smeared on their fingers and lips was a curious gray powder not unlike gritty volcanic ash. A brick-sized package of the stuff was found on the person of the fat woman.

"What do you make of this, Mr. Carter?" Inspector Bhalk said.

Nick Carter shook his head and shrugged.

It was Vashti Takore who had the last word. The beautiful thief had spoken a prophecy and an epitaph when she had laced the sacred Goor with the poison called the Easer of Sorrow:

"Let Kali have what is hers."

DON'T MISS THE NEXT NEW
NICK CARTER SPY THRILLER

BLOOD RAID

Carter glanced up at the moon, an artificial-looking golden ball that was sending a bright shimmering light over several miles of sea behind them and three hundred feet of sheer cliff face in front of them.

At the top, on the very edge of the cliff, was the villa. It was an enormous, rambling, three-story structure belonging to a long-gone colonial era. At the side, coming down the cliff face, a set of narrow steps was cut into the stone.

"It'll be tricky in the moonlight," Hardy said, killing the engine of the launch.

Carter nodded. "That's why I'll go first . . . take the sentries out." According to Mock's intelligence, there were always two, one walking the stone path and one at the top guarding the tall iron gates.

They were drifting now at the headland marking the

approach to the cove. Carter felt the launch roll as Olaf dropped anchor. He looked over at Noreen. She was nervous but she managed a smile.

The AK-47 looked awkward in her hands, but he knew that Hardy had taught her how to use it that afternoon. She would stay in the launch and hit anyone if he managed to elude the team and try for an ocean escape.

"Watch for my signal," Carter said, and rolled over the side of the launch.

He swam effortlessly around the breakwater and struck off across the cove. When he reached the pier, he sidestroked from timber to timber until he felt his flippers hit rocks. Quietly, he pulled himself up clear of the water and shucked the flippers. From the oilskin bag on his back he took his pistol, the Kalashnikov, and the canvas sneakers. When the sneakers were on and tied, he started up the path, staying as low as possible.

The stone path curved like a snake up the cliff face. Halfway up, he heard the soft pad of feet coming down.

Carter accelerated to the curve and dropped flat, holding the pistol in both hands in front of him. His belly did a soft flip-flop when the footsteps stopped.

Then he saw the flare of a match around the curve, heard a fast intake of breath, then a long exhale.

Seconds later the man walked around the curve, the burning glow of his cigarette helping Carter's aim.

The Killmaster pressed the trigger, centered the laser beam a foot below the cigarette's glow, and put two slugs in the man's chest.

The *phhht* sound was still in his ears as he caught the body and eased it silently to the ground. Without a second's pause, he stepped over it and continued his ascent.

Near the top he paused. The villa was dark except for a few lights on the first floor. A scrolled lantern hung just inside the closed iron gates. From the gates to the rear of the house was about fifty yards of garden.

Somewhere in there was the second guard. And then Carter saw him, lounging against a tree just twenty feet inside the gate. He, too, was smoking and gazing up at the sky.

The Killmaster crept forward and balanced the pistol on one of the iron cross-grates. The laser beamed on and he fired once. It was enough, but, just in case, he put two more slugs into the body as it slid down the tree.

Taking a penlight from his bag, he pointed it down the cliff and flashed it three times. Then he went to work on the padlock. Just as it opened, he heard a sound behind him. Running feet . . . bare feet.

Out of the corner of his eye he saw a huge black dressed only in a swimsuit.

It hit him at once. One of them had gone for a midnight swim, and somehow Carter had gotten by him in the water without being seen.

One of the man's powerful arms swung in an arc. Carter saw the glint of moonlight on a long blade, and rolled. At the same time, he kicked out, catching the man in the crotch, deflecting the knife that now swished past his head. A heavy body crashed down on top of him and the man jerked the knife clear as Carter grabbed the thick wrist.

They rolled over and over, locked in a hideous embrace, Carter holding the knife hand, his legs in a death-grip scissors around the black's muscular belly. A free hand went to Carter's throat, a thumb mashing the windpipe closed. They thrashed about on the ground. Carter felt his throat closing, his breathing becoming painful. He yanked at the wrist with his hand, and momentarily the choking eased up. Carter gave a mighty surge, rolling and shoving with his right hand, forcing the knife into the other's chest.

The black grunted and strained. The knife came out

of his chest and he struggled to turn it around toward Carter. Carter twisted again, exerting every ounce of his strength, pushing, pressing, squeezing, then giving a desperate lunge that sank the knife to its hilt a second time in the deep chest. The man screamed once, a scream that turned to a burbling gurgle, and blood spurted up in Carter's face.

Carter staggered to his feet, shaking his head, just as the others hit the top of the path.

—From BLOOD RAID
A New Nick Carter Spy Thriller
From Charter in June 1987

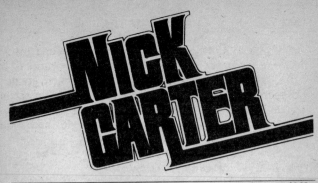

☐ 57291-X	**BLOOD OF THE FALCON**	$2.95
☐ 06790-5	**BLOOD OF THE SCIMITAR**	$2.50
☐ 57281-2	**BLOOD ULTIMATUM**	$2.50
☐ 57290-1	**CROSSFIRE RED**	$2.75
☐ 57282-0	**THE CYCLOPS CONSPIRACY**	$2.50
☐ 14222-2	**DEATH HAND PLAY**	$2.50
☐ 57292-8	**DEATH SQUAD**	$2.75
☐ 21877-6	**THE EXECUTION EXCHANGE**	$2.50
☐ 57294-4	**HOLY WAR**	$2.75
☐ 45520-4	**THE KREMLIN KILL**	$2.50
☐ 24089-5	**LAST FLIGHT TO MOSCOW**	$2.50
☐ 51353-0	**THE MACAO MASSACRE**	$2.50
☐ 57288-X	**THE MASTER ASSASSIN**	$2.50
☐ 52276-9	**THE MAYAN CONNECTION**	$2.50
☐ 52510-5	**MERCENARY MOUNTAIN**	$2.50
☐ 57502-1	**NIGHT OF THE WARHEADS**	$2.50
☐ 58612-0	**THE NORMANDY CODE**	$2.50
☐ 57289-8	**OPERATION PETROGRAD**	$2.50
☐ 69180-3	**PURSUIT OF THE EAGLE**	$2.50
☐ 74965-8	**SAN JUAN INFERNO**	$2.50
☐ 57287-1	**SLAUGHTER DAY**	$2.50
☐ 79831-4	**THE TARLOV CIPHER**	$2.50
☐ 57293-6	**THE TERROR CODE**	$2.75
☐ 57285-5	**TERROR TIMES TWO**	$2.50
☐ 57283-9	**TUNNEL FOR TRAITORS**	$2.50

THE ETERNAL MERCENARY
By Barry Sadler